a STARLIGHT INN novel

Jessica Anne Renwick

Published by Starfell Press

**Starlight Inn Book Two
Novel Dreams**

Copyright 2021 @ Jessica Anne Renwick. All rights reserved.
Contact the author at www.jessicarenwickauthor.com

ISBN (paperback) 978-1-989854-08-2
ISBN (Kindle eBook) 978-1-989854-09-9
ISBN (eBook) 978-1-989854-10-5

Cover design by Ana Grigoriu-Voicu, www.books-design.com
Edited by Talena Winters, www.talenawinters.com
Formatting by Red Umbrella Graphic Designs and Formatting
Proofread by Erin Dyrland
Author Photo © Bonny-Lynn Marchment. Used by permission.

Printed in the United States of America, or the country of purchase.
This book or any portion thereof may not be reproduced or used in any manner whatsoever without the express written permission of the publisher except for the use of brief quotations in a book review.

More by Jessica Anne Renwick

THE STARLIGHT INN

Harvest Wishes
Novel Dreams
Holiday Hopes

Pumpkin Promises

For my loving partner who makes sure my cup is always filled with tea through my late-night sessions, and who has believed in my writing since day one. Thank you. Your support means the world to me.

Chapter One

Anna Simone ran her fingers over the hardcover spines in the urban fantasy section of her favourite bookshop, Steeped in Books, reading the author names. *Santana. Sencha.* She paused, hovering her hand over Sevoy and Sipowitz.

Right here. This is where it would have been. If she squinted, she could almost see her name. If only Raven Stone Press hadn't gone bankrupt, dissolving her contract in the process.

She loosened the wool scarf around her neck, then tore her gaze from the shelf and moved to the women's fiction section next to it. She'd been trying to make the best of the situation, hoping her agent could find a new deal for *The Wicked Moon*.

But Clarissa had warned her that a cancelled manuscript in a waning genre would be tough to sell again.

The smell of patchouli wafted over her from the incense diffuser by the front door. The earthy tones soothed her, reminding her that a bookshop was still her favourite place in the world, even if it didn't hold space for her work. A place to get lost in the smell of books, with the shiny covers depicting magical priestesses or regency lovers or cozy small towns. The promise of new worlds—ones where the main character inevitably wins and the endings are always happy.

An outfacing novel with a woman in hiking gear on the cover caught Anna's eye. She pushed her glasses up her nose, then picked it up for a closer look. The hiker wore a backpack even larger than her torso, and the blurb stated she was on the Inca Trail in the Andes mountains.

Maybe that's what I need. A solo trip. Something to reset my life. She clutched the book to her chest, thinking of her dwindling savings account. *But with what money?*

After moving to Cedar Lake, British Columbia from Calgary, Alberta in July, she'd taken a part-time job helping out in the kitchen at the Starlight Inn.

That had been her plan—to work casually and spend the rest of her time writing. And of course, to live closer to Jace. But now it was early November, and she'd lost the book deal that would afford for her to do that and the boyfriend who'd persuaded her to move there in the first place.

Anna made her way to the front desk, stepping around a couple browsing the science fiction section, and nodded at the clerk. She'd grown to know the staff here over the last few months. They had even planned to host a book launch party for *The Wicked Moon*—another loss that Anna hadn't expected to hurt so much.

The clerk, Laura, pushed the blond bangs of her chic pixie cut from her forehead and greeted Anna at the till. "Hey. Did you cut your hair?"

Anna tugged self-consciously at a black tress that came just below her chin. She'd needed a change, and cutting off seven inches of hair had been both alarming and freeing. "Thanks. It feels weird, like my neck and shoulders are naked. But I'll get used to it."

"I like it. Shows off your beautiful brown eyes." Laura held out her hand. "Find what you're looking for?"

Anna handed her the book. "This one's an impulse buy. You've got to stop ordering so many great titles. I can't help myself."

Laura flipped the book over and read the back. "One woman's journey from rock bottom to the peak of Huayna Picchu. Thinking of going on a trip?"

"I wish," Anna replied. "For now, I better stick to the trail around Cedar Lake. I'm in no shape to climb any mountains."

"I think you could do it. Monty would motivate you," Laura said, referring to Anna's dog.

Anna shook her head, suppressing a laugh. "I'd have to carry him up. We make a good team, wandering through the woods as slow as turtles." She had recently adopted the lovable retriever-mix from the local animal shelter, Pawsitive Match. Though his most active years had passed, the old dog had stolen her heart the moment she'd met him.

Laura squinted at the book's price and tapped the numbers into the antique, metal cash register. Anna had no idea how the clackety old machine could be reliable. But it was part of Steeped in Books's charm, along with the smell of herbs, the disorganized shelves, and the baskets of loose-leaf tea behind the till.

Everything about the shop was whimsical and fun—exactly like its owner, Christine Walsh.

Laura tapped a button on the machine, and the cash drawer sprang open with a clang. "That'll be twenty ninety-eight."

Anna tried to hide her wince as she pulled her debit card from her bag. Laura took it from her and shoved the cash drawer closed with her hip.

It's just twenty bucks. I'll hit the library next time. Or read one of the dozens of stories on my eReader. Anna took the book from Laura and stuffed it in her tote bag. "Thanks."

"Come back any time." Laura pointed to a flyer taped to the top of the counter. The image of a book with a red bow tied around it stood out in the middle of the paper. "In fact, you should come by our book club meeting this Friday. We're picking a Christmas novel to read. Joanne Peters is vying for a classic like *A Christmas Carol*." She glanced around the room, as if Joanne might be hiding behind a bookcase, then leaned forward and whispered, "I anonymously suggested *A Merry Murder*, that new mystery. We do a boring classic every year."

A knot formed in Anna's stomach. She'd been scheduled to read an excerpt of *The Wicked Moon* for the club this winter. The last thing she wanted to do was join as a reader, at least until the sting of her loss resided. Her face grew warm at the thought of the stares she'd receive walking through the door.

Twenty-six years old and already the town's failed author—knocked from her precarious pedestal. I bet everybody in the book club is talking about it.

"Umm, I'm not sure. Maybe. That mystery sounds good, though."

Laura gave her a sympathetic look. "Think about it. It's a lot of fun, even with the constant bickering over what to read."

The curtains behind the counter swept open. Christine rushed out with the plum-coloured fabric of her gauzy dress flowing behind her. Her copper-coloured waves—interspersed with natural grey—nearly reached her waist. "Anna, I thought I heard your voice! I have this new tea for you to try. It's from a local company, they blend everything right here in the Fraser Valley."

She grabbed a basket from the shelf behind her and set it on the counter, then pulled a paper bag from a drawer beneath the till and began to fill it with pungent dried leaves. "It's a green variety, mixed with white peony and rose petals. I tried it last night. It's lovely."

Anna tugged on the strap of her tote bag. "Oh, Christine—"

"It's on me." Christine passed her the paper bag, now bursting with fresh loose-leaf tea. "When I took my first sip, I immediately thought of you. Notes of soft florals and delicate jasmine. Warm like a spring breeze."

Anna tucked a choppy lock behind her ear and adjusted the arms of her glasses. That did sound good. How did Christine know that green tea was her favourite? "Well, thank you. You really don't have to."

Christine rounded the front desk and shoved the tea into Anna's bag.

Laura tapped her fingers on the till, a wry smile on her face. "I don't think you have a choice."

"You deserve it, dear." Christine squeezed Anna's arm affectionately. "Please, let me know how you like it." She paused. "Anna, you're still part of the Steeped in Books family. And when your agent finds your story a new home, we will throw you the biggest party you can imagine."

Anna swallowed, touched by the woman's kindness. "Thank you. That means a lot. I'll keep you updated." Tears welled in her eyes, and she fought the urge to bolt from the store. "I should really get going. Monty needs to be let out. Thanks for the tea."

"Any time, dear."

"Hope to see you soon," Laura added.

Anna gave them an awkward wave, then walked stiffly to the entrance and pushed through the door. A blast of cold autumn air hit her face, and she pulled her scarf over her cheeks. From the look of the dark clouds above, rain was on the way. Soon.

"Anna!" A familiar voice called from behind her.

She turned around. Sophie, Christine's daughter and the head chef at the Starlight Inn, stood beside her grey Civic parked in front of the bookshop. She closed the driver's side door and joined Anna on the sidewalk.

"Cold, isn't it?" She tugged at the collar of her wool peacoat, then hugged her elbows. "It's like Halloween ended and winter blew right in."

"I almost froze on my walk with Monty this afternoon." Anna shivered and balled her cold fingers. "Heading inside to see your mom?"

"Yes. She's got some tea she wants me to serve at work," Sophie replied. "It's only earl grey, but she insists it's special for some reason. The hints of bergamot perfectly match the inn's vibe—or something like that."

"Ah. She just gave me some green jasmine that reminded her of me."

"Of course, she did," Sophie replied with a knowing smile. She shifted her purse strap higher on her shoulder. "Anyways, I'm glad I caught you. I was going to call you tonight. Are you looking for more work hours?"

"Yes!" Anna bit the inside of her lip, trying to dial back her eager tone. "I mean, I have lots of time now. Did Katie take on another event?" Their boss, Katie Hoffman, had been working hard to expand the inn's potential over the last year. Between weddings, festivals, and hayrides, the Starlight Inn had become a cornerstone of the community.

"How did you guess?" Sophie tilted her head, her green eyes bright with humour. "The Cedar Lake Christmas tree lighting is in a few weeks, the last Saturday of November. They want to make it a big event this year and have a dance afterwards."

"And we're hosting it?" Anna asked. "Are we renting a tent like we did for the Fowler-MacKenzie wedding?" Other than a handful of quaint cabins and the stable behind the Victorian-style inn, the only other building was a ramshackle barn in one of the horse pastures. Anna assumed it had last been used decades ago, probably for milking cows.

A cold wind whirled around them, blowing a mass of Sophie's copper-coloured waves over her face. She swiped it aside with a gloved hand. "No, the old barn. We're fixing it up—finally! Think of the weddings we can hold there next summer." She clasped her hands. "Katie needs people to clean and set everything up. You'd be paid your usual wage, plus any overtime."

"I'm in," Anna replied. Sweeping and dusting weren't exactly in her repertoire, but how hard could it be? And the extra money would give her more time to figure out what she was going to do. "You know, I've never been to an old-fashioned barn dance before."

"After seeing the wedding Katie planned, I'm sure it's going to be beautiful," Sophie said with a note of yearning in her voice. "Twinkle lights, flowers, a live band…" Another whip of icy wind hit them, and she shuddered. "I better get inside before we blow away.

I'll let Katie know you're on board. Maybe come in a bit early tomorrow to talk to her?"

"Sure thing." Anna nodded. "See you tomorrow."

With a tinkling of chimes, Sophie rushed inside the store.

Sophie and Christine, they're both so good to me. The two women had gone out of their way to welcome Anna to the community. Between Steeped in Books and the Starlight Inn, she'd made better friends here than she'd ever had in Calgary.

Despite her mother pushing her to move home, she wanted to stay. She'd grown to love this town in the Fraser Valley of British Columbia. The lush trees and mountain lakes, the fields of sunflowers in September, and the dappled horses at the inn—they felt like home. The quiet setting was the perfect place for her creative spirit. Much better than the bustling urban centre of Calgary.

She ducked against the wind and crossed the street to the Blooming Box floral shop. Arrangements of bright orange and red flowers filled the store's front window. Anna gazed at them wistfully, then opened the door on the edge of the building and trotted up the stairs to her one-bedroom apartment.

Monty greeted her at the entrance, with his tongue lolled to the side and his shaggy tail a flurry of wags.

"Hey, buddy." She cradled his face and kissed his nose, then hung her tote bag on the hook next to the door. "Need out before it rains?"

He bounced on his front legs in reply, and she grabbed his leash from the coat hook and snapped it to his collar. She glanced at the looming, grey clouds through her living room window, then patted Monty's head.

"Maybe things will work out. I've got friends here. And I've got you." The patter of rain sounded on the roof. Anna guided the dog into the hallway, her mind turning to her manuscript. *I'll go back through Clarissa's notes. Now that I have a bit more time to figure out my money situation, I can focus on rewriting that story to fit what publishers are looking for now. I got a deal before. I can do it again.* Her stomach squeezed. *Right?*

Monty let out a whine and tugged at the leash. Anna snapped back to reality, locked her door, and allowed the dog to lead her toward the stairs.

"We'll have some more late-night writing sessions, buddy," she told him. *Like when I first wrote* The Wicked Moon, *squeezing in every second I could around my work hours back at the restaurant in Calgary.* "If I work hard enough, I can fix this. Everything will be okay."

Chapter Two

Matthew Talbot heaved a box of red potatoes into the back of his brother's truck and settled it against the side. Rain drummed on the roof of the old shop, and a gust of cold rushed in from the open overhead door. He zipped up the canvas jacket he'd borrowed from Marshal, then grabbed the pen from the clipboard resting on the tailgate and checked off the potatoes.

"This isn't so bad," he tried to convince himself. *A little physical labour never hurt anybody. And it beats sitting inside, staring at an empty email inbox and willing editing clients to show up. Right?*

The thought of his old job made his stomach knot. Only a few months ago he'd been on top of the world—a great apartment in Toronto, a junior editing gig at a small publishing house, a girlfriend who looked like a supermodel and worked for the same publisher. Then out of the blue, the company's CEO announced the publishing house was closing its doors—immediately. Two days after Brittany had ended things with him.

Matthew scowled and grabbed his travel mug from next to the checklist, then sat on the tailgate to take a drink of hot coffee. *Now here I am, back in Cedar Lake, digging turnips for my older brother.* He wasn't sure where to go next. Editing jobs were few and far between, and while he was grateful for a decent severance package, it hadn't been enough to afford his rent in Toronto for long. So, he went home to Cedar Lake to figure out his life. Stuck living with Marshal and trying to scrounge up freelance editing gigs.

Wind whistled through the trees outside. Matthew shivered, then took a satisfying swig of dark roast goodness. *It's only temporary. I'll figure something out.* He always did. And for the most part, living with Marshal had been fun. It was almost like they were teens again, watching sports and playing video games together. *When he isn't stressing over this flipping farm, that is.*

Marshal marched into the shop, water dripping from his ball cap, and shot Matthew a look. "Got the yellow onions loaded yet?"

"Aye, Captain." Matthew tipped his mug in his brother's direction. "Onions, potatoes, turnips, beets. Everything Sophie wanted for the inn tomorrow."

Marshal picked up the clipboard and skimmed the list. "And the salad boxes for the school's lunch program?"

"All there." Matthew hooked his thumb toward the full truck box with *Morning Harvest* painted on the side in golden letters.

Marshal flicked his gaze to the boxes, his lips moving in a silent count.

A flicker of irritation ran through Matthew. "Dude. I said I'd do it, and I did."

Marshal furrowed his brows and tossed the list on the workbench against the wall. "You missed a box of parsnips yesterday."

"I did? Sorry." Matthew ran his free hand through the top of his wavy brown hair, which was cut in a stylish fade. *How did I miss that? I swear I checked the list at least three times.* He glanced at his surly brother, pushing down the hint of annoyance in his chest.

Two years older than him and born four minutes before their sister, Madison, Marshal had always assumed the role of the responsible older brother. Matthew had grown up in his shadow, joining Beavers when he was five like Marshal had, and following his big brother all the way to Scouts. Despite his objections, their parents had insisted on it, pointing out how much Marshal loved the program. But Matthew wasn't his brother. While Marshal had taken on leadership roles and meticulously planned hiking and rafting trips, Matthew had spent most of his time goofing off with his friends.

Now, he set his coffee on the tailgate. "Who did I miss on the order?"

"Josie's Diner," Marshal replied. "One of our best customers. Better bring her something extra to make up for it. Maybe some of those red gold spuds. She always needs more potatoes."

Matthew winced. *Of course, I had to mess up the order from one of his favourite clients.* "I can run them to her first thing while you talk to the contractors."

Marshal grunted and gave him a nod. "Thanks."

He pushed back his hat and rubbed his forehead with his arm. "Those contractors—I swear that greenhouse is going to be the death of me."

"It's going to be the death of us all," Matthew said dryly. The whole project had turned Marshal from his usually good-natured self into a total grump.

Matthew glanced out the overhead door. The unfinished greenhouse stood next to the shop, its steel arch-frame standing starkly in the dark and rain. The polycarbonate sheets for the covering were supposed to arrive next week. But Marshal had been on the phone earlier with the supplier, his face the colour of a ripe tomato. Like everything else, something must have gone wrong. After fighting with the town to get proper licensing, another electric pole had been erected in the farmyard last week. One that Marshal hadn't expected to need. Now with this rain, there was no way the electrician could come out tomorrow to work on the wiring.

And of course, Marshal was in a rush to get the greenhouse done before winter hit. He'd been in a crusty mood since Matthew moved in a couple weeks ago. The only person who'd been able to make him smile lately had been Sophie, his childhood friend now-turned girlfriend and head chef at the Starlight Inn.

Marshal scrubbed his face with his palm and sighed. "Look, I'm sorry. I know it's been stressful around here, and your life isn't exactly a walk in the park right now either."

Matthew raised a brow. "It's not that bad." He paused. "You know, aside from losing my job, having to move to the other side of the country, an ex-girlfriend who won't lay off—" his tongue stiffened.

Marshal leaned his back against the workbench. "I never liked her, you know."

"You met her like what—twice?" Matthew replied. He had no idea why he was protecting her. Sure, things hadn't been great between them for months. But did she have to start dating Frank McDavin? His ex-boss—the guy Matthew needed for a reference? His stomach clenched at the thought.

"Twice was enough," Marshal replied. "She wasn't exactly warm to us last Christmas."

"Let me guess, you didn't like her big-city pant suits?"

"Nah, her pant suits were fine. It was more like her attitude. She called Mom's job *cute*. What's *cute* about being the town's event planner?" Marshal shook his head. "She looked down her nose at us from day one."

Matthew thought of the way she'd laughed at Cedar Lake with disdain and told him she'd never move there in a million years. *Maybe he's right.* "Well, she's gone now. Out of my life for good."

"Then why is she still calling you?"

Matthew's neck grew rigid, and he rubbed the back of it. "I don't know, Marsh. To let me know how happy she is with Frank? I haven't been answering her. She's not begging me to take her back, that's for sure." *She'd made it perfectly clear that we were done. That she needed somebody more sensitive—like Frank, I guess.*

They were silent for a moment, then Marshal cleared his throat. "Well, I'm glad you're home. We missed you around here."

"Wow. All it took was some wallowing to soften you up?" Matthew grabbed his coffee and got to his feet. "I should have started complaining weeks ago."

Marshal rolled his eyes, then clapped Matthew's shoulder. "Want to help me with the delivery for the inn tomorrow? Beena can take the load to the school," he said, referring to his only farmhand. "You can see what the Hoffmans have done with the place, and say hi to Sophie and Mads."

"I could do that." Matthew set his mug on the workbench, then closed the truck's tailgate. "It'd be fun to see Madison in action at her new job." His sister had moved back to Cedar Lake a month before he did. After finally leaving Vancouver and her abusive marriage, she'd seemed to settle in quickly to their old hometown. By the time Matthew had arrived, she'd already gotten a new job as a bookkeeper at the inn and had reconnected with her old boyfriend, Dylan Stewart—who also happened to be Marshal's best friend.

He frowned at the thought of her ex-husband, Jamie. He'd never liked the guy, none of their family had. But he'd had no idea how bad it had gotten. If there had been any clues, he'd have been home long before now. Instead, he had avoided his family for months, embarrassed by his own problems.

He had a lot to make up for—to Madison, Marshal, and his parents. That was why he was out here, loading crates of vegetables into the back of a dirty farm truck.

Marshal stepped around him and gave the truck box one last check. "I think we're set for tomorrow morning. Let's head in."

Matthew pulled the hood of his jacket over his head and followed Marshal through the rain and across the yard to his old two-story farmhouse. Built in the 1950's with an add-on front porch, it was the definition of quaint and simple. But it had been kept up well over the years and with its rustic exterior, it suited Marshal perfectly.

They entered the porch and kicked off their boots, and Matthew hung his jacket in the closet next to the freezer. "Got time for some *Fallout*?" he asked, referring to a video game they'd been playing together.

"Nah, I'm beat," Marshal replied. "I'm hitting the shower and going to bed."

Matthew gave him a crooked grin. "It's nine o'clock, old man."

Marshal let out a laugh and made his way to the hallway, then glanced over his shoulder. "Some of us have to be up at six. Including you, if you're going to get those boxes to Josie first thing."

"Did I promise that?" Matthew rubbed his chin, and followed his brother up the rickety stairs that led to two bedrooms. Marshal had converted the bedroom on the main level into his office. Luckily, he'd had a spare for Matthew to move into while he figured out what to do with his furniture in storage in Toronto.

Marshal stopped at the top of the stairs. "You just did, and there's no backing out now."

"Yeah, whatever." Matthew waved him off, hoping to get a rise from him. "Well, 'night then. I'm going to check my email. Maybe a magical manuscript fairy graced my laptop with an editing client."

Marshal snorted. "Good luck with that." He grabbed a towel from the linen closet, then made his way downstairs to the only bathroom.

Matthew chuckled and entered his sparse bedroom. A twin bed in the corner, a blue paint-chipped dresser he recognized from their childhood, and an old elm nightstand that probably came with the house. After his modern, walnut bedroom set with high-thread count sheets, he felt like a college kid again living with whatever free stuff had been handed to him.

His stomach twinged, but he pushed the thoughts aside and grabbed his laptop from the top of the dresser. He flopped onto his bed, then set it on his lap and opened it.

The only new email sitting in his inbox had a subject line that read *Read me!*. The sender: Brittany Holt.

Now she wants to email back and forth? No way. He closed the laptop and set it on the nightstand, his stomach churning. He had nothing to say to her.

He got up from the bed, slipped off his sweater, and hung it in the open closet next to hangers filled with Marshal's checkered shirts. His mouth twitched as his gaze lingered on the closet, a familiar ache in his chest. He'd left Cedar Lake at eighteen to strike it out on his own, to show his parents and everybody in that suffocating town that he *could*. That he wasn't going to follow his brother's footsteps or the path his parents had laid out for him—trade school at a local college because aside from English, his grades weren't good enough to be a doctor like his dad.

He jerked the closet door closed, worried that his worst nightmare was coming true. *If I don't get a new editing job soon, am I going to morph into a flannelled mini-Marshal and start delivering pumpkins around the countryside?*

Chapter Three

Anna blinked back tears as she sliced the red onion on the plastic cutting board before her. She tapped her foot to the pop song playing over the inn's kitchen speakers, lost in thought about the notes her agent had sent her about her book. Clarissa wanted to remarket it as a young adult novel. *If I age Rowena down to seventeen and make some tweaks to the romance aspect, maybe it could work.* She bit the side of her cheek. Should I rewrite it in first-person narrative? *I'll check with Clarissa tonight.*

With her mind still wandering in the fae forest of her story, she lifted the cutting board to slide the sliced onions into the glass salad bowl. But before she could deposit the vegetables safely into the bowl, she banged the cutting board on the bowl's edge, and the onions tumbled to the countertop and onto the floor.

Sophie's voice jerked her to attention. "Everything okay there, Anna?" From her spot on the other side of the island, she placed one last salmon fillet into the pan in front of her, not even glancing at Anna as she spoke.

Tad Hoffman, the twenty-two-year-old son of the owners of the Starlight Inn and Sophie's assistant, madly whisked a pot of sauce on the stove behind Anna. His russet brown skin glistened with sweat, and he rubbed his forehead with the crook of his elbow. "She's daydreaming again. Must be a good one. Probably about books? Or dogs?"

Anna sighed and scooped the onions from the countertop into her hand. "Ugh. Sorry about that. Tad's right, my head is in the clouds today."

Sophie wiped her hands on her apron and gave her a sympathetic smile. "It's not a big deal. Toss them in the compost and grab another onion." She flicked her gaze to Tad. "Do you have the glaze ready?"

"I'm on it." Tad set down the whisk, then grabbed the pot and rushed to Sophie's side. "This is possibly *the best* honey garlic glaze I've made yet.

I can't wait to see the look on old Henly's face when he tries it," he said, referring to his instructor at the culinary school he attended in the evenings.

Anna strode to the compost bucket that sat open next to the sink and dumped her handful of onion inside it. She grabbed the broom from the cupboard and began to sweep up the mess on the floor, barely registering the conversation around her. *Do I really want to change* The Wicked Moon *for a younger audience, though? I'll need to rework Rowena's job, education, her relationship with her mother—I'll need to change so much.*

Sophie's voice cut through her thoughts. "Well, your teacher picked a good night to come in to see how your apprenticeship is going. Honey glazed salmon, roasted herbed veggies, Mediterranean salad—we'll knock his socks off!" She paused. "What do you think, Anna?"

"Um—" Anna swept the remaining pieces of onion into the dustpan and straightened. "Totally. You're going to ace this, Tad."

Tad peered over Sophie's shoulder at the salmon. "I hope so. Henly's known for being tough. He's a real Gordon Ramsay."

"He can't be that bad. Nobody's *that* awful in real life." Sophie picked up the pan and balanced it in her arms. "Is the oven set?"

"Warmed up and ready to go." Tad adjusted his hair net over his tight black curls, then glanced at the clock. "Almost four o'clock. Good work, team. As long as Anna gets those onions under control, we'll be ahead of schedule."

"Consider them controlled." Anna dumped the dustpan into the compost box, then returned it and the broom to the pantry and grabbed another onion from a box on one of the ledges. She returned to the island and set the vegetable root down on the cutting board. Carefully, she sliced it in half, then set down her knife and peeled away the top layers.

Sophie squeezed by her, balancing the pan in her arms. After placing it in the oven, she peered out the window above the sink. "Oh, good. Marshal's here with today's order. I was worried he'd be late. He's been working so hard on that greenhouse, and it's been nothing but problem after problem."

Tad leaned his elbows on the counter. "Have you convinced him to take that little vacation yet?

The weekend getaway you mentioned, to that cabin in the Okanagan?"

Sophie rolled her eyes, her hands on her hips. "Trying to convince him to take a break from work is like…" she paused, biting her lip.

Anna and Tad exchanged glances, and Anna raised a brow. "Like trying to convince you to take on one less catering event?"

"Oh, stop it." Sophie crossed her arms, but her lips twitched with a repressed smile.

A frantic barking that sounded much too close to the inn met Anna's ears. Sophie leaned over the sink for a better look out the window. "Anna, those goofy dogs are out again."

Katie and Rodger graciously allowed Anna to bring Monty to work. Madison, Marshal's sister who worked as their bookkeeper, brought her lovable Great Dane every day too. They usually stayed in the wire kennel attached to one of the stable's run-in horse stalls. Dane, the stable manager, had welcomed the idea and even set them up with dog beds inside the barn. It was the perfect arrangement. That is, until one of the mutts learned how to get out.

Anna grabbed the kitchen towel hanging from one of the drawer handles on the island and wiped her hands, leaving the half-chopped onion on the cutting board. "Oh, those dogs!" She gave Sophie an apologetic look. "Again? Last Thursday, the Tuesday before that, and now this? Dane must be out with the horses. I don't know which one figured out how to open that latch, but we need to get a chain for it. I'll go deal with them. Sorry, Soph."

Sophie waved her off. "No problem. We'll figure out how to contain those furry beasts yet."

"My bet's on Mack as the culprit," Tad said. "He was roaring around here this weekend. And Monty's too sweet to do such a thing."

Anna snickered and made her way to the back door. "Too sweet or too old?" She kicked off her Sketchers and pulled on her rubber boots.

Tad tapped his chin, then shrugged. "Probably both."

She grabbed her navy-blue rain jacket from the hook by the entrance and slipped it on, then pulled open the door. A bone-chilling breeze swept over her, but the rain had let up to a slow drizzle. She flipped her hood over her head, then made her way down the steps to the parking pad.

Marshal approached her with an armload of boxes filled with vegetables. Water dripped from the brim of his hat as he gave her a curt nod. "Hey, Anna."

"Hi, Marshal," she replied. "Sorry about the dogs."

Marshal grunted, then shot her a wry grin. "They're all over my helper back there," he jerked his head toward the truck box. "Mind putting them away?"

"On it," she replied cheerfully.

"Thanks." Marshal started up the steps to the inn's back door.

Anna made her way around the side of the truck, cringing at the sound of Mack's booming bark. She imagined he was jumping all over Beena, Marshal's usual farmhand.

But instead of Beena's petite figure, Anna found a man in a canvas jacket scratching Monty's ears behind the open tailgate. His back to her, he let out a whistle and Mack thundered toward him with a big stick in his mouth.

That is definitely not Beena.

"Come on, boy!" With his ball cap and broad shoulders, he looked like Marshal from behind.

"Umm, hey," Anna said, catching his attention.

"Sorry about the dogs, they're supposed to be up at the barn."

At her voice, Monty bounded toward her. When he reached her side, he shook his wet coat and splattered her with muddy water.

"Monty! Sit!" Once the overeager canine complied, she wiped at the mud on her jacket.

The man looked over his shoulder and gave her a wide smile, revealing a dimple in his chin. Her pulse quickened as she met his hazel eyes. She faltered, her hand on Monty's head, unsure of what to say.

"No problem," he said. Mack reached him, legs wobbling like a newborn foal's, and banged the stick against his legs. "Ouch, dude! This one's a bull in a china shop." He wrestled the stick from the tawny giant, who then bounded away excitedly with drool stringing from his jowls.

"Oh, yeah. That's Mack. He's a handful," Anna replied. Her hood had slipped low over her glasses, and she pushed it up and away from her face. "You're sure good with him."

He wound back with the stick and threw it across the lawn in Mack's direction, then sauntered over to her.

"That's because we're buddies. I'm Matthew, Madison and Marshal's brother." He held out his hand.

"Oh, Madison mentioned you were in town." She took his firm hand and gave it a shake.

"In a good way? Or in a *my pain-in-the-butt brother's back* sort of way?" He shoved his hands in his pockets, an amused look on his face.

"Well, you know Madi—"

Marshal's voice cut through the air. "Hey, dog whisperer, you bringing that variety box in or what?" He stood with the door half open, gesturing toward the truck.

"Give me a second, old man!" Matthew called back. He gave Anna a sheepish look, then slid a box filled with vegetables from the truck box. "I better get this inside."

Mack galloped up to them with the stick in his jowls, and Anna grabbed his collar. "Well, it was nice to meet you. I'm going to wrangle these dogs back to the barn."

Matthew shifted the box, his gaze lingering on her. "Good luck with that. Don't let Mack push you around."

"Dude!" Marshal called out again. "Cut the chit-chat. Let's go!"

Matthew shook his head and started toward the inn. "Why are you so ornery today?"

Anna smiled at their brotherly banter. Mack twisted and pulled against her hand, trying to follow Matthew.

"No way, buddy." She wrestled the stick from the dog's mouth and tossed it into the trees, then whistled for Monty to follow her. Quickly, she made her way to the barn with the dogs and put them inside the kennel, making sure to properly latch the gate.

She strode into the stable and just as she had thought, there was no sign of Dane. She grabbed a spare lead rope that was looped around the bars of one of the stalls, then returned to the kennel and tied it securely around the gate posts. *There. That should keep them in for now.*

As she made her way back to the inn, she noticed Marshal's truck was still there. Her stomach fluttered, thinking of Matthew and the way he'd handled the dogs, hoping she'd get a chance to properly introduce herself.

She dug her fingers into her palms. *What are you thinking, Anna Simone? No guys. Remember?*

After the Jace debacle, she'd promised herself she'd stay away from dating for a while. Her heart still pinched when she thought of her ex-boyfriend and his shaggy blond hair, his soulful eyes and the way he had made her feel like somebody important. They'd met in an online writing group and after dating long distance for a few months, he'd convinced her to move to Cedar Lake. And then he promptly dumped her two weeks later for his ex-girlfriend from Rocky Ridge, the next town over.

She reached the kitchen steps and swallowed the tightness in her throat. *I am definitely not ready for handsome men with adorable dimples.*

She pushed open the door and stepped inside, then lowered her hood and patted down her stray locks. The music had been turned up, and Matthew leaned on the island with his back to her. Marshal and Sophie were nowhere to be seen—probably gone to see Katie about something to do with the menu.

The pantry door hung open, and Tad's voice came from within it. "So, Sophie said you're an editor?"

Anna paused, her fingers on the zipper of her jacket.

"Oh, yeah," Matthew replied, still facing away from her. "Or, I *was*. Before the publishing house folded. They sent me and everybody else packing a few weeks ago."

Anna's stomach clenched at his words. *That can't be right...*

"So now you're Marshal's right-hand man?" Tad asked.

Matthew snorted. "More like his errand boy." He paused. "To be honest, I'm glad for the break, though. Things were tense those last few months at Raven Stone."

Anna dropped her hand from her jacket.

From the pantry, the sound of something tumbling on the counter met her ears. Tad's voice quivered. "Er—Raven Stone?"

"Yup. What a nightmare." Matthew shifted his weight and crossed one ankle over the other. "They pulled me over to help the acquisitions editor choose which books to take with him to his new job. And which ones to cut. Talk about pressure. At least I wasn't the poor schmuck who had to notify all the agents."

Tad poked his head out of the pantry, frowning. "Wait, you picked which books got canceled?

From *Raven Stone* publishing house?"

Matthew scrubbed his face with his palm. "Yeah. Obviously, a lot of those manuscripts weren't up to snuff anyways. I don't know what Ahmed was thinking when he proposed them to the marketing team. But still, it wasn't easy."

Anna felt as if she'd been punched in the stomach. A lump formed in her throat. She took a step back and bumped against the door.

Tad finally noticed her, and his eyes grew wide. "Anna—"

Matthew looked over his shoulder, and he lit up with that same charming smile he'd given her earlier.

Anna wanted to wipe it from his smug face.

He straightened and smoothed a hand over his jacket. "Oh, hey. How'd it go with the dogs?"

Her pulse thrummed inside her. She grabbed the door handle and pushed it open. "I, uh, forgot something. At the barn. I have to go."

Before either of them could say anything more, she dashed outside and closed the door behind her. She thumped down the steps through the misty rain, her mind reeling. *He worked for Raven Stone?*

He canceled The Wicked Moon? *How can he be here, in Cedar Lake, of all places? And Madison Talbot's brother!*

Her rubber boots squelched against the soggy wood chips on the trail, sounding much like her heart felt—damp and squishy.

What am I supposed to do now? Pretend like he doesn't exist in front of Sophie and Madison every day at work? And act like I didn't just flee the building like a scared rabbit?

She reached the dog kennel and pressed her palm against her forehead. The sweet smell of fresh hay from the pole shed next to the stable met her nose. Monty and Mack greeted her, dancing in front of the wire door. She frowned, remembering Matthew playing with them earlier.

His words in the kitchen circled her mind... *a lot of those manuscripts weren't up to snuff anyways. I don't know what Ahmed was thinking...*

Anna let out a groan. *And to think, I thought he was cute.*

Matthew closed the tailgate of Marshal's truck and rounded the box to make his way to the passenger door.

Marshal was still finishing up inside, and Matthew had gone out to double-check the order for the next drop-off. Now finished his task, all he had to do was wait.

Before he could open the truck door, a flash of navy-blue caught his eye. Sophie's assistant emerged from the trail in the trees, and he raised his hand to wave at her. "Hey!"

She kept walking, staring at the ground.

A frown tugged at his lips, and he lowered his hand. She trudged up the steps and went inside the inn.

Did I do something to offend her? He pushed back his ball cap and scratched his forehead. *What's her name again? Tad called her Anna, I think?* He would have to ask Marshal later. It was strange that she'd ignored him. But maybe she hadn't heard him call out to her. After all, when she'd first come out to deal with the dogs, she'd seemed friendly enough. He thought of her shy smile, and the way her pretty brown eyes had widened when he'd greeted her.

For a minute, he'd thought she'd been flirting with him. Maybe even hoped she'd been.

Don't flatter yourself, Talbot. He shook his head, then opened the truck and slid into the passenger seat.

The way she bolted when she saw me in the kitchen later—he buckled his seatbelt. *It doesn't matter, anyways. I have no time for flirting or dating or anything like that. Not right now.*

He slid his phone from his pocket and brought up his email, then eyed the unread message from Brittany. *Nope. No time or energy for women right now.*

He scrolled up to see a new email from Editors Canada, reminding him to complete his freelance listing on their website. He tapped the link and began to fill in the form, grateful for the distraction.

Chapter Four

Anna crossed her legs and glanced at Monty, who sat at her feet with his ears perked. She had just loaded her plate with pizza, poured a steaming cup of the green tea from Christine, and sat at her kitchen table to have dinner with her older sister, Kelsey.

They'd made this their Monday night ritual after Anna moved away from Calgary—a weekly Simone family virtual dinner. Although recently, it had been a sisters-only event. Their mother hadn't joined them for over a month now. As the Vice President of an oilfield construction company, Vanessa Simone was always busy with late-running meetings or client dinners.

Anna opened the video app, waiting for Kelsey to appear. She tapped the tabletop impatiently, staring at the potted mums peeking over her laptop screen. She'd bought the fiery orange flowers from the shop below her apartment, hoping to add some cheer to the drab autumn weather. She'd read that they symbolized optimism and joy, something she sorely needed lately.

Monty let out a whine, with his grey-haired muzzle twitching in anticipation. Anna tore her gaze from the flowers and picked a piece of pepperoni off her pizza and offered it to him. He sniffed it, then gently took it from her fingers and padded to his bed in the corner of the living area.

Kelsey appeared onscreen. She set down her wine glass, slipped the scrunchie from her wrist, and pulled her long ash-brown hair into a messy bun.

"Hey, Kels," Anna said. "Did you get my text?"

"I sure did." Kelsey patted the bun, peering into the corner of the screen which Anna assumed held a little box that mirrored her. She then dropped her hands and stared directly at Anna. "So, let me get this straight. An editor from Raven Stone—no wait, the editor from Raven Stone *who canceled your book*—is from Cedar Lake, and you work with his sister?

And his brother dates the chef? Unbelievable, Anna. This could only happen to you."

"I know." Anna eyed her steaming plate of pizza. The cheesy goodness usually made her mouth water. But tonight, the thought of food made her sick to her stomach. "I overheard him talking about it to Tad, and I panicked and ran away. Like a child. I'm sure Tad put two-and-two together and told him who I am." She thought of Matthew's cocky grin and frowned. "What a mess. What am I supposed to do now?"

Kelsey gave her a sympathetic look. "You've always been a runner, Anna. Every time conflict happens—"

"I know." Anna winced. Her sister was right. Ever since they were kids, any time a situation became tense, she was gone. Especially whenever their grandmother came over and inevitably got into an argument with their mom—usually about the way Vanessa was raising the girls. Anna would rush to her bedroom and get lost in one of her books. She'd push her emotions aside, hiding away until the voices gentled and the coast was clear to return downstairs.

Kelsey continued, "I mean, it's not like you have to see him all the time. I would carry on as usual.

Aren't you starting on that barn project this week anyways?"

"Yeah, tomorrow," Anna replied. Katie had confirmed everything with her that afternoon, after Anna had returned to the kitchen with her shattered pride. She would work on the barn during the morning, then have a few hours to wash up and come back for her late-afternoon kitchen shift. "The extra cash will be nice. And maybe I can lay low and steer clear from Madison for a bit."

"Oh, Anna. I don't think you need to avoid her." Kelsey tilted her head. "Hey, remember when I went on that disastrous first date with Rachel's cousin?"

Anna picked up her tea and warmed her cold fingers around the mug. "Who's Rachel again? Another call agent? I don't remember anything about you dating her cousin."

"Yeah, we sit side-by-side." Kelsey shuddered. She often complained about her job in the busy call centre, cramped in a cold basement office with a dozen others, talking to upset clients all day. "My date with Dave was horrible. He got drunk, was rude to the waitress, and suggested that we *dine-and-dash*." She picked up her wine glass and rolled her eyes. "Obviously, I paid the bill.

I told the girls at work about it, and he turned out to be Rachel's cousin."

"Yikes." Anna blew on her tea, then took a sip, enjoying the smooth flavour. "How did you deal with that?"

Kelsey let out a laugh. "Honestly, Rachel knows how he is. She agreed with me, and we never talked about him again."

"I doubt Madison and Sophie are going to agree with my feelings about Matthew." Anna sighed. "Madison talked about him for days before he came home. And Sophie made him a welcome home cake. They adore him."

"He's their family, of course they love him," Kelsey replied. "But think about it. Madison's his sister. If he's as big a jerk as it sounds like, she'll know. I mean, you said he was bragging about rejecting books he didn't think were any good. That seems like grade-A jerk material to me."

"That is rude, isn't it? Like he took pleasure in the act of tearing others down." Anger flared inside Anna, and she thumped her mug on the table. "His attitude wasn't professional at all."

"Exactly. Don't get hung up on it. He's just like all those big business guys—only out for himself." Kelsey straightened in her chair. "You'll get another contract. You did it once. You can do it again."

"Right. I'm working hard on those notes Clarissa sent me. I can make *The Wicked Moon* catch another publisher's eye." Anna nodded, but an inkling of doubt rolled through her mind. Their mother hadn't been very supportive. Her response to Anna's news had been a curt email—*We all knew this was a pipe dream, Anna. Time to grow up. Move home, and I can help you find a real job.*

"Kels?"

Her sister looked up from her glass. "Yeah?"

"But what if I can't? Maybe Mom's right. She said—"

"Don't you listen to her for one minute." Kelsey pointed at Anna through the screen. "Just because she made it her mission to climb the corporate ladder doesn't mean we have to. Trust me, I get it. She's not exactly thrilled with me either—the vet school drop-out."

"At least you have the option to move up in your company," Anna replied. "I'm a kitchen assistant and a failed author who moved to a new town for some guy who dumped her immediately after." She lowered her voice.

"What if that jerk editor is right? What if my book isn't good enough? What if he tells Madison and Sophie, and they feel sorry for me?"

"You're overthinking this." Kelsey began to count on her fingers. "First off, you already said you're working with your agent to strengthen the book. She's obviously got some faith in you. Second, who cares if Mr. Pompous Editor tells Madison and Sophie that your book isn't good enough? Do they seem like the judgmental type? From what you've told me, they've been nothing but nice to you."

Anna adjusted her glasses and took a deep breath. "I know. You're right. It's not all bad." She picked up her tea and took another sip to calm her nerves. "I can do this. I can fix *The Wicked Moon*. And I have a new story I'm working on too. I started plotting it last night and did a rough draft of the first chapter."

"Good." Kelsey leaned back in her chair. "Keep writing. Keep trying. You did it once, you can do it again. Seriously, don't give up on your dreams."

"Like you did?"

"Hey, my dreams are a different topic. And it's off limits." Kelsey pressed her lips together. "Now, tell me more about this new book you're writing."

"It's about two sisters." Anna's stomach growled, and she pulled her plate toward her. "One's really sweet and kind, but the older one's pretty bossy."

"You mean, she's a good leader," Kelsey replied. "If you're writing an autobiography, I need to edit all the stuff about me."

"And let you rewrite our history?"

"More like ensure you depict me as the ever-supportive and saintly sister that I am."

Anna giggled, her tension easing away. Maybe Kelsey was right. The situation with Matthew might blow over without any drama. *I'll only have to see him once in a while, when he delivers produce with Marshal. I can manage that. It's not like I work with him every day.*

She pushed all thoughts of him from her mind and picked up a slice of her pizza. "So, my new story idea involves these estranged sisters who go on a trip together to hike Machu Picchu."

The early morning sun shone through the bare branches of the hemlock trees that surrounded the stable, warming

Anna's back. She closed the dog kennel behind Monty, watching as he and Mack bounded toward each other in greeting. Well, Mack bounded, and Monty shuffled. The horse lead rope she'd put there the day before was wrapped around the kennel post, and she tied it in a slip knot around the gate's latch. *That should keep them in.*

She started down the path toward the back pasture, humming to herself. After her talk with Kelsey last night, her mood had lifted. So what if her co-worker's brother was involved with Raven Stone's closure? It wasn't her fault. Besides, she would never have a reason to talk with him about anything other than vegetables.

She tucked her hands in the pockets of her down vest, happy to be wearing something other than her usual kitchen slacks and tunic. After working in the barn this morning, she'd have a couple hours to run home and get ready for her shift in the kitchen. It would be a long day, but a good one.

And later, she could focus on fixing *The Wicked Moon*. She'd been up past midnight the night before, with Monty lounging next to her on his fluffy bed, going through Clarissa's notes on how to make her main characters younger. And tonight, she'd do it again.

The old barn stood in a stand of trees, surrounded by long brown grass and dried thistles. Its rough wood-slat sides were grey with age, but the structure appeared solid enough. Its new tin roof glinted in the sunlight, redone this summer when Katie had noticed the old stuff peeling away after a storm.

Rodger's farm truck, a beat-up red Chevy, sat in front of the structure with three people gathered around it. Anna immediately spotted Katie, appearing completely out of place in her fashionable plum-coloured pantsuit that flattered the dusky tones of her skin. She stood next to the truck's tailgate with her husband, Rodger. He nodded at Anna and pushed back his ragged ball cap to reveal tight salt-and-pepper curls that matched the grey of his whiskers. A teenage girl who looked as if she could be their daughter stood on his other side.

Just as she greeted them good morning, a shiny red two-door car pulled up and parked next to the truck. The driver's door opened, and Matthew Talbot stepped out and shot her a dimpled grin.

Anna's throat went dry. *What's he doing here? You can't tell me he's helping with the barn too!*

"Hi, Matthew." Katie waved him over to the group. "You're right on time. This is our niece, Violet. Lucky for us, she's homeschooled and has her mornings free to help."

"And I wanted some extra cash," Violet added.

"Yes, a bit of payment helped entice her to join us," Katie said. "Anyways, I think you met Anna yesterday in the kitchen." She gestured to her husband. "Rodger is about to go over our game plan."

You've got to be kidding me. Anna moved to the rear of the truck, standing as far from Matthew as possible. He tried to catch her eye, but she focused her attention on Rodger.

Katie's husband ambled to the barn door and leaned against the frame. "As you can see, it doesn't need any structural work. It was gutted about ten years ago to store hay in the winter, but we cleared it out last spring and built that pole shed by the stable to use instead." He gripped the metal handle of the sliding door and heaved it to the side. The rusty rails groaned in protest, but Rodger gave the door a good shake and another pull, and it rolled open just wide enough for a person to walk through.

Katie cleared her throat. "A new door is on the list."

Rodger peeked through it, frowning. "Yep. I've already ordered the parts from Beth Dawson," he said, referring to the owner of a hardware store in town. He waved his hand at the dust motes that floated in the beam of light in the entryway. "We've got some heaters coming next week to install too, but first up, the whole barn needs a cleaning. A good one. There's some old milking equipment in the back room that needs to go too."

Anna let out a breath, making a note to suggest they split into teams to tackle the chores. *Girls versus guys. There's no way I can work alone with him.* Her stomach roiled at the thought of working closely with Mr. Pompous Editor, as her sister had dubbed him.

She snuck a sideways glance at him, and he gave her an easy smile. With his navy-blue hooded sweatshirt and Canucks ball cap, he didn't look so pompous today. But he hadn't at first yesterday, either.

"Well," Katie put a hand on her hip, "it sounds like you've got everything covered, Rog. I better take off. I have a bride and her mother coming for a tour of our venue in a few minutes." She gave the barn an appraising look. "Maybe they'll see the potential in this place for the wedding reception. Once it's cleaned up, it'll be better than a tent."

They said goodbye, and Katie started across the field toward the driveway that led to the inn. Anna had no idea how her boss managed to walk so gracefully across the soft pasture in her high heels. She scuffed the toe of her sneaker in the dirt, grateful she didn't have a job that required dress shoes and suits.

Violet straightened one of the straps of her denim overalls, then made her way around the vehicle and peered over the tailgate. "Well, let's see what we have for supplies."

Rodger rejoined them, then dug the keys from his pocket and tossed them toward Anna.

"Oh!" She fumbled, but managed to catch them with the tips of her fingers. "What are these for?"

Rodger hooked a thumb in the direction of the building. "It's dustier than a John Wayne movie in there. If we're sweeping out floors and rafters, we're going to need masks." He nodded toward Katie, who strode purposefully up the driveway toward the inn. "I'm not quite as organized as my wife."

Violet leaned over the side of the truck box and began to rummage through the contents. "Better add garbage bags and another good broom to the list. Uncle Rodger, I thought Tad would have helped you get everything ready."

"You want me to run into town?" Anna asked, gripping the bottle-cap keychain. She peered in the passenger window. Sure enough, a gear lever stood out in front of the bench seat. "I can't drive a standard."

Matthew stepped forward with an eager look on his face. "I can do it. I've been driving stick forever. Dad made us kids learn how."

"Bill's a smart man." Rodger nodded as he slid his wallet from his back pocket. He opened it and pulled out a credit card, then handed it to Anna. "You go with him and handle the money. It's a company card, so be sure to bring the receipt."

Anna tried to return the card to him. "Why don't you go with him? Violet and I can get started cleaning out the old equipment." *Please!*

Rodger waved her off. "Nah, you better go. There's an old milk tank and some pipes in there that'll be too heavy for you girls alone." He joined Violet at the back of the truck and gave her a fatherly tap with his fist on her shoulder. "We'll get going on it. Head into Beth's, she'll give you a better deal than the big box store."

"Sounds like a plan," Matthew said with an all-too-lofty smile. "Need anything else?"

"See anything to add to the list, Violet?" Rodger asked.

By now, Violet had already unloaded the sparse amount of supplies Rodger had brought and set them on the ground—two big brooms and a milk crate filled with cleaners and tools. She put her hands on her hips, looking even more like Katie than before. "I think we're set. Before we need paint, anyways."

Anna relented and put the card in her vest pocket, then handed Matthew the keys with a sinking heart. *Great. Just awesome. So much for not being alone with the guy who dashed my dreams.*

Matthew jangled the keys cheerfully. "Alright. We won't be long." He motioned to Anna. "Coming?"

Anna gritted her teeth, trying to ease her racing pulse. "Yeah," she turned to Rodger and Violet. "See you in a bit."

"See you later." Rodger gave them a wave. "Don't forget those masks."

"We won't." Matthew hopped into the driver's seat and turned on the Chev's engine with the rumble only a worn-out old truck could have.

Anna sucked in a breath, then opened the passenger door and climbed inside. Matthew revved the engine playfully. She pressed her lips together and flicked on the radio, hoping to avoid any small talk on the drive to town.

Chapter Five

Matthew cringed at the peppy pop song playing over the radio, then stole a sideways glance at Anna. She sat pressed against the side door as if ready to bail out of the truck at any second. He scratched his chin, wondering what happened to the friendly demeanor she'd had when he first met her the day before.

"Mind if I change the station?"

She shifted, looking uncomfortable, and gestured at the radio. "Go ahead."

He turned the dial to a local rock station, changing the all-too-cheerful song to a familiar hard beat. He shot Anna a grin. "Much better! Are you okay with this? What kind of music do you like?"

She shrugged. "I'm fine with whatever."

Okay. Not so talkative today.

They reached the end of the driveway, and he turned the truck onto the gravel road and shifted gears. He had to admit, driving the old Chev was fun. He hadn't driven a truck like this for years. And the quiet country roads were almost therapeutic compared to the busy streets in Toronto, surrounded by honking horns and aggressive morning commuters. It reminded him of his childhood, bouncing around in his dad's truck or cruising as a teen with Owen and Ryan in Owen's old Chevy Sprint.

The song ended and a commercial promoting Cedar Lake's tree lighting came on. Matthew cleared this throat. "That barn doesn't look like much now, does it? But I think once we spruce it up, it'll be pretty nice. My mom is the town's event planner—"

"I know," Anna said, staring out the window. "Madison told me."

"Oh, yeah. You two are friends, right? She told me your name's Anna. We never had a proper introduction the other day."

She nodded, keeping her gaze on the fall foliage out the window.

What is with this girl? I haven't had this cold of a reception since I almost forgot the carrots for the Johnsons last week. That scowl on Marshal's face when he checked the boxes—he shook his head.

If Anna and I are going to work together, this ice needs to thaw. "So, Madison said you like books, and you're a writer? Me too. Well, I'm an editor." He paused. "In my real career, I mean. This is temporary, until I find another job."

Anna picked at a loose thread on her vest pocket. "Um. Yeah, I guess I like reading."

"What genres do you like?"

"Oh, you know. A bit of everything."

A hint of irritation rolled through Matthew, but he pushed it down. They were silent for a moment, an AC/DC song thundering over the speakers, and he cranked off the radio. "Did I do something to offend you? When I was at the inn yesterday with Marshal, you ran out of that kitchen faster than a cat on a mouse."

"What?" Her eyes widened. "N—no. I just don't know you."

"Are you always this uptight with new people?

Because at first, when I was playing with the dogs, you didn't seem so shy."

Her cheeks grew pink, and she pushed her glasses up her nose. "It's weird, isn't it? The whole book thing."

"What whole book thing?" He thought of what Madison said about Anna's book deal getting canceled. *She can't be a Raven Stone author. That's crazy.* But the way she looked at him with those big brown eyes, as if he were the one who destroyed her world... "You—you're not associated with Raven Stone Press, are you?"

She swallowed and dipped her chin. "Madison didn't tell you?"

"She didn't say you were with *Raven Stone*." He bit back a groan. *What are the odds of two people with the same press in Toronto being from the same small town in southern BC?* He held his tongue, his mind reeling. *Okay. This isn't a big deal. It's just business. But how did she—* "You overheard me talking to Tad yesterday, didn't you? About it being my job to help pick which books to cut? That's why you left."

Anna's cheeks grew even redder, and she nodded again. If she sank any further into that seat, she would disappear between the cushions.

"Okay," he said, thinking back to his conversation with Tad. Maybe the way he'd said things had been a bit cruel. But he never thought that one of the authors could be standing right behind him. "I'm sorry if I came off as a jerk. I didn't mean to. I didn't know you were involved."

Her brows knit together. He could have sworn her eyes were glistening with angry tears.

Panic rose inside him. *Is she gonna cry? No, dude, fix this. Fix it now.*

"Look, Anna," he said, trying to make his words sound soothing. "It wasn't personal. That's just business. Authors lose contracts all the time."

She lifted her chin, her tears replaced by angry defiance. "*Just business*? It's not *just business* for writers. Do you know how hard it is to even get an agent?"

His chest hitched. He wasn't sure if it was from the way she looked, sitting there staring at him through those long lashes, or from the guilt that rose inside him. "Yes, but—"

"And then to land a book deal? It takes years!" She crossed her arms, but her scowl melted and she bit her lip.

"Okay," he said, his throat tight as he forced his gaze away from her and back to the road. "I know how hard it is. I'm sorry if I sound flippant—"

"Flippant? It sounded like you enjoyed dashing people's dreams."

"What? No," Matthew stammered. *Get a hold of yourself, man. She's not the first beautiful woman to get mad at you, and she won't be the last.* "That's not true."

The truck jolted over a washed-out section of the road, bouncing both him and Anna from their seats. After righting himself, he tugged his jacket straight. "Sorry. I should have slowed down."

She pressed her lips firmly together and readjusted her seatbelt.

They approached the highway in silence, and he shifted gears to roll the truck to a stop at the intersection. "I didn't enjoy making those cuts. And I'm not usually in charge of acquisitions. I only did line edits there." He put the truck in neutral and twisted in his seat to look at her. "Ahmed had a job lined up with another press, but he could only take five books with him. My boss had me help him go through the manuscripts.

A lot of the books we'd already acquired didn't make it. Yours isn't the only one."

She scowled. "I know it wasn't. You let a dozen of us go."

He pushed back the brim of his ball cap and rubbed his forehead. "Look, you can hate me if you want. But it wasn't personal. I didn't even read your book, only the proposal. I don't even know which one it was."

Her shoulders relaxed as she leaned against the seat and crossed her legs. "Okay. I get it. It was *just business*. But you sounded so darn smug about it."

"Smug?" He raised his brows, letting his gaze linger on her bowlike lips. "I'm not smug about anything. It's not fun knowing that I'm partly responsible for crushing all those authors' dreams—your dreams." He paused. "Besides, it's not like I was expecting to run into one of you in *Cedar Lake*. What are the odds?"

She took a deep breath, then tucked a lock of hair behind her ear. "Technically, I'm from Calgary. I moved here in July." She waved her hand in a dismissive gesture. "But that's not the point. You're right. It is weird. When I heard you talking to Tad—well, that's why I've been uncomfortable."

"Fair enough," he replied. "But if we're going to work together, I think we should try to get along. We don't have to talk about the book stuff. Truce?" he held out his hand for her to shake.

She eyed his fingers as if they might bite her, but then a slight smile crossed her face. She placed her smooth hand in his and shook it. "Alright. Truce."

He dropped their handshake and shifted the truck into gear, then looked down the road for oncoming traffic. "So, what kind of music do you *really* like?"

Anna tilted her head. He pulled onto the highway, and she leaned forward to play with the dial on the radio. "Definitely not metal."

"I figured." He chuckled as she turned the dial back to the pop station. A man's throaty croon floated from the speakers. "Ed Sheeran? Really?"

She smirked and leaned back in her seat. "Did we agree to a truce or not?"

"Right." He gave her an exaggerated eye roll, and she laughed. He liked the way it sounded, as if she had at least partially lowered the drawbridge of the fortress around her.

For a moment, he admired the flush of her cheeks and the way her glasses sat crooked on the bridge of her nose.

As if reading his mind, she caught his eye and pushed them higher.

He averted his gaze to the road in front of them, relieved they'd worked things out. At least, sort of. He'd never dealt with a jilted author before. As a line editor, he'd never had a say in any of the contracts. At least, not until Raven Stone's closure. He hadn't given much thought about the people whose dreams he'd helped ruin. He'd told himself exactly what he had told Anna—it was the way things worked in the publishing business.

But now that he was faced with seeing another person hurt by the company's closure, he wasn't sure how to deal with it. The pain on her face had been apparent—and he hated that he'd been one to cause it. He racked his brain, trying to remember which manuscript had been hers. Maybe he'd been too quick to judge.

He tapped his fingers on the steering wheel, wondering if he should say more. Maybe he could offer to help fix her manuscript and shop it around, but the thought of it made his stomach queasy. The urge to say something to make her like him pulsed strongly within him. And nothing good could come from that.

No, it's better to leave it alone. He shifted the truck into a higher gear, then stole another glance at Anna from the corner of his eye. She caught his gaze and her lips curved with a small smile, causing his pulse to quicken. He swallowed. *Seeing her every day for the next few weeks is going to be weird enough.*

Chapter Six

Anna slid the tray of dishes into the Starlight Inn's dishwasher, closed the door, and hit start. Her back stiffened as she straightened, every muscle aching with fatigue. With a sigh, she slipped off her rubber gloves and lay them on the counter. Through the window above the sink, the stars shone brightly in the dark sky. *A perfect night to set up my laptop and get lost in a fairy world.*

Tad came out of the walk-in pantry with two loaves of bread. He shoved aside the fruit bowl on the kitchen island and placed the bread next to it. Dinner had ended a couple of hours ago, and they'd just finished cleaning the kitchen. Sophie had gone to Katie's office to discuss the menu for the community dance.

Tad covered his mouth with a yawn, then gave Anna a sympathetic look. "How are you doing, champ? You had a long day—sweeping an entire desert from that barn, and then your shift in here. You must be beat."

Anna stretched her arms above her head and let out an appreciative groan. "I'm alright. Tired, but it's only for a few weeks."

By the time lunch had hit, she'd been coated with grime and dust. She'd had to rush home to shower and change before returning to work in the kitchen. There'd been no time for a proper break, and she hadn't spent this many hours on her feet in years. She longed to go home and curl up on her couch with Monty and her laptop. She had a fae world to rebuild, and several hours of sweeping a rough wooden floor had given her plenty of time to reconstruct it in her head. *I need to tone down the violence in that battle scene. Maybe I should talk to Clarissa about what's appropriate for teens—*

"Anna?" Tad snapped his fingers in her direction. "You home?"

She jerked to attention. "Sorry, I have a lot on my mind. My agent gave me a ton of notes on *The Wicked Moon*. She's going to pitch it to YA publishers."

Tad cocked his head. "YA? From what you told me this summer, Rowena is struggling with her new career and a red-hot, off-and-on relationship with a gnome. That doesn't sound like a book for teens."

"A gnome?" Anna picked up a dish towel from the counter and hung it over the handle of the stove. "No, Eamon is a leprechaun."

Tad raised a brow. "Oh, pardon me. Because a leprechaun is *much* different than a gnome."

Anna laughed and leaned her hip against the counter. "It sounds cooler in the book, I promise. But you're right about the audience issues. I have a ton of work to do to make it appropriate for YA readers. And good enough to catch the interest of a new publisher." The thought of her rejected manuscript crept into her mind and with it, Matthew's scathing words from the day before. "Apparently, it's not very impressive at all. At least, not to certain editors."

Tad leaned his elbows on the island and propped his chin in his hands. "Yeah. About that. I saw Matthew pull in this morning. Dad said he's helping with the barn project."

Anna's neck grew warm. "Yep. Your dad even sent me to town with him, first thing."

"Ugh, Dad." Tad buried his face in his palms. "He is so unobservant. I'm sure he had no idea how uncomfortable you were around Matthew."

"What do you mean?" Heat rose to Anna's cheeks. "I'm not uncomfortable—"

Tad straightened and began to sort through the flyers on the counter. "Oh, I see. You bolted away from here yesterday because you enjoy hanging around outside in a freezing cold downpour, then?"

Anna crossed her arms. "Okay. Maybe it's a bit awkward. I mean, I never thought I'd have to meet the man who rejected my book proposal. Much less work with him."

"Did he say anything to you? Does he know who you are?" Tad asked.

"He knows now." She thought back to the truce she and Matthew had made that morning in the truck as they rumbled to town. *Why does he have to smile like that?* She bit the side of her cheek, remembering his earnest explanation and desire to clear the air.

Tad paused from his sorting. "What did he say?"

"He offered an olive branch, and I took it. And then—well, he was so *nice*."

After picking up supplies from the hardware store, they'd driven past a retro-looking ice cream shop she hadn't been to yet. She'd let it slip how much she missed going for rocky road with her sister. Matthew had turned the truck around, insisting they had time to grab a couple cones. As they drove back to the inn, happily eating their frozen treats, he'd told her stories about going to that shop with his family as a child. How Marshal had always insisted on plain vanilla, while Madison had loaded her sundaes with every kind of candy available.

"And your favourite is honestly rocky road? The same as mine?" Anna had asked him, gesturing to his cone with hers in disbelief.

He had given her that crooked grin, then taken a lick of his ice cream. "Always has been. Guess we have more in common than we thought."

Tad's voice jerked her back to the present moment. "What's wrong with him being nice? You said that like it's a bad thing."

"It's not. Or, I don't think it is. I don't know." Anna tore the hairnet from her head, catching it on an arm of her glasses. She took them off and pulled the hairnet free, then shoved it in the pocket of her trousers.

Tad regarded her for a moment, as if deciding if he should say more. "He probably didn't mean what he said to me about those books not being any good. He seemed nice enough otherwise, and we all say dumb things sometimes."

"I guess that could be true. But he's confusing. One minute he's a pompous jerk, the next he's Mr. Wonderful." Her mind reeling, Anna began to clean her lenses with the corner of her tunic. "What's his angle? Is he really not so bad, or is he only trying to win me over with that boyish charm?"

Tad tapped the flyers on the countertop, then gave her a catlike grin. "Boyish charm? Was he flirting with you? I mean, he's pretty cute—"

"What? No." Anna put her glasses on and narrowed her eyes at him.

The swinging doors that led to the dining area opened, and Madison entered the room. "Who's cute?"

"Nobody," Anna replied.

Tad grabbed one of the stacks of flyers and tossed it in the recycling bin beneath the counter. "Oh, some guy Anna's been ogling."

"Who? I want in on the juicy gossip." Madison flipped

her wavy dark hair over her shoulder and stepped up to the coffee maker on the counter. She motioned to the empty pot and wrinkled her nose.

"It's nobody. Just some guy I saw in town."

"Speaking of guys," Madison gave Tad a sideways look, "how are things going with you and Ethan? Did you go to that hockey game with him on Saturday?"

Tad picked up the dishrag from the counter and began to wipe down the surface. "I did. And even though I hate sports, we had the best time. I never thought I'd enjoy sitting in a packed stadium, eating poutine and drinking weak beer."

Madison let out a little squeal. "That's amazing! You two have been flirting for ages. It's about time."

"Don't tell anybody yet. We're trying to keep it on the down-low. You know, with him working here with the horses, and my mom is technically his boss—it could be awkward with my parents."

Anna gave him a wide-eyed stare and lowered her voice. "You never told me you two finally went on a date."

Tad stopped cleaning and rounded the kitchen island to the sink. "You never asked. You're always off in la-la land, thinking about fairies and books."

He's right. I've been so wrapped up in my own problems lately. "I'm sorry."

Tad playfully snapped the rag in her direction. "It's okay. You've got a ton on your plate, between men and books…"

"Speaking of books," Madison flicked her gaze to Anna, "I was going to ask you, was your book with that publisher my brother Matthew worked for? Raven Stone, right?"

Tad snorted, then turned on the tap and began to rinse out the rag.

Anna blinked, her stomach tight. "Umm, yeah. It was. Why do you ask?"

Madison shrugged. "I talked to him this morning and put two-and-two together. From what he's told me, the Canadian publishing world is small."

Anna swallowed the lump in her throat. She adjusted her glasses, trying to appear nonchalant. "Uh, yeah. He mentioned today that he used to work for Raven Stone. Small world is right." She forced a laugh, one that rang too high and she hoped didn't sound fake.

Tad gave her a mischievous glance over his shoulder.

Madison opened the drawer beneath the coffeemaker and began to rummage around inside it. "Well, that's really too bad Raven Stone went under. I bet you two can share some battle stories."

"Yeah, maybe." Anna pointed at the coffee pot. "Are you thinking of making more coffee? At this time of night?"

Madison pulled out a filter and closed the drawer. "I know, I shouldn't. But I'm so tired, and I still have a few hours of bookkeeping ahead of me when I get home. Setting up Dylan's new company has been more work than I thought." She paused. "Why did I offer to do his books and administration stuff?"

"Because you love him," Tad replied. "And since he gave up his job in the city to stay here and start his own computer company—"

"IT consulting business." She shoved the filter in the coffeemaker, dumped in a package of ground coffee, and hit start. "And you're right. I'm so glad he's staying here. It'll get easier once everything is set up and rolling. I hope."

"It will." Anna nodded, relieved she'd managed to change the subject. She slipped off her apron and hung it on the hook on the pantry door.

She checked the chicken-shaped clock on the wall above it. "It's eight-thirty already. I should get going. I have lots of work to do too." She wiggled her fingers in a typing motion.

"Sounds good, Anna. See you tomorrow." Madison replied. "Oh, and once you grab Monty, don't forget to tie that rope around the gate again. I still have to get to town and get a proper chain."

"Of course."

"Good luck with the edits," Tad said. He lowered his voice. "And with you-know-who tomorrow morning."

"Who?" Madison asked.

"Nobody." Anna shot Tad a daggered look, then went to the door and pulled on her jacket. "Have a good night, you two."

She stepped outside, enjoying the cool breeze against her hot cheeks, then closed the door behind her. She trotted down the steps toward the stable to grab Monty from the dog kennel. Just as her feet hit the wood-chipped path, her phone vibrated in her jacket pocket. She stopped and pulled it out, then squinted at the screen.

A text from her mother blinked at her. *King Construction is hiring several data-entry clerks. I emailed you the link for the application. You wouldn't be working in my department, so there's no conflict of interest. Call me, and we can discuss you moving home if you decide to apply.*

A second later, another text popped onto the screen.

I highly suggest you apply, dear. It's a foot in the door, and you don't have many options right now, do you?

Anna frowned. She could practically hear her mother's condescending tone. She had never supported Anna's move to BC, and as soon as Anna and Jace had broken up, Vanessa had given her the *I told you so* speech.

Losing her book deal had only been another reason for her mother to push her to move back to Calgary and get a *real job*. Anna shuddered. The last thing she wanted to do was live with her mom, even for a few months while she found a new place. And she had zero desire to climb the corporate ladder, which would give her even less time to write.

No, she wanted to be an author. To make a living connecting with people through her stories and sharing her creativity. Giving people an escape from the everyday stresses of life, a fantasy world to slip into even when times were tough. That's what she was meant to do, she could feel it inside her. And she'd been so close. She'd had a taste of it, and she wanted more. She needed to rewrite her book and get it published.

I'll answer her later. Anna shoved her phone in her pocket and started down the path. *After I get my work done on* The Wicked Moon *tonight. If I can get this book right, Mom would lay off. She'd see that I can do this and make my own success.*

I can put in the work and do these edits—even if it means completely changing the story.

Chapter Seven

Matthew's breath steamed in the early morning air as he lowered the tailgate of the old red Ford truck. A dozen beat-up antique milk canisters stood in rows inside the box, some with dented sides and rust lining the edges of others. Marshal had picked them up the evening before from the Johnsons' farm for their mom, Paula, and Matthew had decided to take the spare truck to drop them off for her on his way to the inn.

He figured he'd leave the canisters on the patch of brown lawn next to his parents' shed and be off, but the sound of a door banging closed came from the log house behind him. He turned and called out a greeting to his mom, who walked toward him with a hitch in her step, still in her fluffy pink housecoat and a pair of rubber boots. Dolly, her white toy poodle, pranced at her side.

"Mom, are you okay? Why are you hobbling along like a lame horse?" Matthew asked.

She reached his side and ran a hand through her cropped grey hair. "Oh, it's nothing really. I had an incident at Christine's yoga class last night."

"Yoga?" Matthew cocked his head. "Wait, doesn't she run the bookstore?"

"Yes, but she has a yoga teacher who comes in on Tuesday evenings," Paula replied. "It's more of a beginner class for us old ladies who are intimidated by the studio downtown. And we have tea after. It's quite nice."

"So how exactly did you injure your leg doing beginner yoga?" He remembered the yoga class in Toronto that Brittany had taken him to, which mostly involved laying in a *corpse pose* listening to wind chimes. "Don't you just sit there, pretending to meditate?"

She gave him an exasperated look and waved her hand. "No, dear. That's not all we do. I was attempting to do a shoulder stand, and I fell."

"That seems—" he paused, biting back the word *ridiculous*— "a bit advanced for you."

She straightened her shoulders and tightened the belt of her robe. "It's not. I've been doing yoga for a few months now. But I'm fine. I only twisted my ankle a bit." She peered around him at the contents of the truck. "You brought the milk cans! They're perfect."

He pulled one of the canisters to the edge of the tailgate and patted the top. "Marshal grabbed them last night. Where do you want them?"

She wrapped her housecoat tighter around her, then walked unsteadily toward the shed with Dolly at her heels. "Your father made room in the shed. They can stay there until tonight when the girls come over to help me clean them up." She pulled a set of keys from her pocket and unlocked the door. "They're going to be fantastic decorations for the Starlight dance. We can take off the lids and put dried flowers in them—"

"Mom, you sure you should be hobbling around like that?" Matthew gripped the closest canister's handle and heaved it to his side. "What did Dad say about your ankle?"

"Oh, you all worry too much. I'm fine." She shooed Dolly aside and pulled open the shed door. "Do you like the name, Starlight dance? It lets people know right away where it's at, and it suits the theme of the Christmas tree lighting and our transition from autumn to the holidays."

"Umm, sure. It sounds great." Matthew entered the dim shed, the only light coming from the window. His dad had taken out the lawn tractor and moved it, probably into the garage. Their tools and yard supplies were lined in organized fashion on the shelving units, exactly like his father's clinic in town.

He shook his head. *Nothing changes around here, does it?* His parents were the only people he knew who had a spotless shed and a leafless lawn, even in November. Their hobbies had always consisted of cleaning and nitpicking the yard. As a kid, his Sunday afternoons had been filled with yard work. Not he'd minded that much. Chore time had always faded into games of tag or hide-and-seek in the trees that surrounded the property, he and Madison goofing off while Marshal complained that they needed to get back to cleaning out the compost bin or whatever job they'd been tasked with. He chuckled at the memories, then set the canister next to several neatly coiled hoses, and returned outside.

His mom stood at the tailgate, eyeing the canisters with her hands on her hips. "What time do you have to be at work?"

Matthew strolled up next to her. "Eight. Why?"

"We better get these unloaded quickly, or you're going to be late."

He glanced at his watch. "It's only seven-thirty, Mom. I've got more than enough time."

She narrowed her blue-eyed gaze at him. "You should always be at least ten minutes early. Maybe even fifteen. It's only your second day on the job."

Annoyance sparked in Matthew's chest, but he pushed it down. *She's just worried.* Exactly like she was when he was fourteen and failed one math exam, and she spent the next three months hovering over his shoulder as he studied.

He took a deep breath, then rocked back on his heels and gave her a crooked grin. "Come on, Mom. I worked for a professional publishing house for four years and always managed to make it on time."

She gave him an irritated look, then reached into the truck box and tried to pull one of the canisters toward her. It caught on the ridge between the tailgate and the truck box and rocked precariously.

"It'll be quicker if I help. You don't want to look bad to Rodger and Katie, or your other coworkers." She paused. "Speaking of which, Madison mentioned to me that one of the inn's kitchen workers is an author at Raven Stone. Or at least, was before the closure. Have you met her?"

"Yeah. She's working on the barn project too."

He thought of how Anna had finally softened and given him that smirk when she'd changed the radio channel in the truck yesterday. And before that, her big brown eyes boring into him as if he were her enemy. He hated that she didn't like him. That she held a grudge, and maybe had a good reason to do so.

He'd been trying to think of ways to make it up to her, to make her feel better about working together. So far, all he could think of was offering to help edit her manuscript. That would mean spending more time with her. Getting her email address. Maybe even her phone number. He shifted uneasily at the thought.

As appealing as all that sounded, he wasn't sure if he was ready to get that close to somebody he found so attractive. After what Brittany had pulled... *I'm overthinking this. Anna's nothing like Brittany. I could tell that right away. And what's wrong with being friends?*

Paula clucked her tongue. "That's too bad. The closure has affected so many people." She adjusted her grip on the milk can and tried to slide it again.

"Hey, let me get it. Okay?"

She jerked on the milk can, and it tipped toward her. She fumbled, but Matthew stepped forward and caught it before it could fall.

"Mom, it's not a big deal. I'll be on time. And if I start running late, I'll give Rodger a call so he knows what's up. We're only working on cleaning out a bunch of old farm equipment."

Paula crossed her arms, looking like a pink tea kettle about to boil with her flushed cheeks.

Matthew sighed and rubbed his chin. *I should have left it at "I'll be on time". But seriously, I'm an adult. She doesn't need to get after me as if I'm a teenager with my first job.* He straightened the canister, then lifted it from the truck. "It's all good, Mom. Don't worry so much."

Paula's face fell. She uncrossed her arms and tightened the tie of her housecoat. "I can't help but worry, Matthew. You took off across Canada—at eighteen no less—to make it in the big wide world. And we thought you did. We were so proud."

Matthew's back stiffened and he adjusted the milk can to hold it with both hands. "And what, now you're not? Because the company I worked for went under?"

"No. I didn't mean that," Paula replied. "But when things fell apart, you pulled away from us. You wouldn't answer your phone. You gave us one-word answers to our texts, if you replied at all. And living so far away, we had no idea what was going on."

Guilt and humiliation washed over him like a wave crashing into rocks. "Well, I'm here now, aren't I?"

"Yes, and for that we're thankful. But we haven't really talked about what happened, and what you want to do now. Your father and I want to help you."

Matthew clenched his teeth, holding back the words in his head. *I can't deal with this right now. Like she said, I have to finish up here and get to work.*

He started toward the shed, swallowing his wounded pride. "You're already helping, Mom. Just welcoming me home while I work things out is enough. Everything's fine. I promise."

Her words gnawed at him. He had to do something more about his career, and soon. But local editing jobs didn't exist, and he didn't want to move across the country again. He'd missed his family. Sure, there might be some options in Vancouver or Seattle, but he'd been scouring online job listings and hadn't seen anything he was qualified for yet.

If I could make a real go as a freelancer, I could work from anywhere. I could stay close to home. Maybe get to know Anna better... But starting a freelance business was no easy task.

He deposited the canister inside the shed. When he returned to the truck, his mom was wrestling with another one on the tailgate. Dolly danced around her feet, barking at the milk jug as if it were about to attack.

"Let me get that. Watch out for Dolly!" He quickened his pace, but she gave the canister a yank and it tumbled into her arms.

She stumbled backwards to right her balance, but her ankle gave out. Dolly leapt out of the way as she fell to the gravel below, landing on her hip. With a painful yelp, she let go of the canister, and it rolled to the side.

"Oh, Mom!" Matthew rushed to her, gravel crunching beneath his boots as he ran. He knelt next to her and placed his hand on her shoulder. "Are you okay? Don't move."

She rolled onto her back with a groan. "I—I think I'm okay." She pushed his hand away and sat up. "Oh, my hip. I think I bruised it."

"And your ankle?" Matthew asked.

"It's sore, but I think I'm okay." She tried to get to her feet, but stumbled. Matthew grabbed her arm and eased her to a sitting position.

"I'm going to help you up and get you into the truck. We need to get you checked out, okay?" She gave him a pained look, and he continued, "Just in case. You don't want to make it worse and end up not being able to help out with the dance."

She closed her eyes and set her jaw, but nodded. "Okay. Fine. But Dolly—"

"I'll bring her inside. Let's get you up and into the truck first, okay?"

"Okay."

He helped her to her feet and let her lean on him as she limped to the truck, wincing with every jolted step.

As he opened the door for her, he gave her a teasing smile. "Looks like I'll be calling Rodger to let him know I'll be late, after all."

Paula heaved a sigh, but got in the passenger seat and leaned it back. "Let's get this over with."

Chapter Eight

Anna picked up a shiny blue hardcover from the shelf before her, breathing in the smell of cinnamon and cloves from the bookshop's diffuser. She tapped her fingers on the glittery gold title, *The Whisper of Wings*, then turned the book over. Even that simple movement made her arms ache, and she winced. The four hours of sweeping and hauling garbage bags filled with debris that morning were already catching up with her. Once Rodger had decided to call it a day, she'd rushed home to shower and change so she would have time to pop into Steeped in Books before heading back to the inn.

She bit her lip as she read the book's blurb. The fairies in her story seemed more devious than the angelic-looking creature with flowing blond hair and shimmery green wings on this cover. But Clarissa had suggested that Anna read some new YA releases about fairies to spark her inspiration.

Princess Auralia must lead her troops against the demon army threatening to invade her land—nope. Anna sighed and returned the book to the shelf. *Too much like an epic fantasy. My story's modern, not medieval.*

She mulled over a few other titles in the section, but there weren't many that fit her exact genre. Most of them were stories about princesses, knights, and fairy worlds of long ago. Sure, they sounded like interesting reads, but they were not good matches for *The Wicked Moon*. There was no way she could completely shift the era. With all the other changes Clarissa had suggested, she would have to write a completely different book.

Her mind wandered to her new work in progress about the two sisters and their journey across the Andes. *Maybe that's what I should do. Scrap the whole book and focus on my new project.* She chewed the side of her cheek, a scene about a bear encounter rolling around in her mind. But Clarissa specialized in fantasy.

Would she even be willing to look at something else? Or would Anna have to start completely over, sending out dozens of queries and waiting for months for a single reply?

She shook the idea from her mind. *Not yet. I only have a couple chapters written, anyways.* She glanced at the counter, where Laura was deep in conversation with an older man wearing a tweed jacket and fedora. *Maybe she knows of a book they can order for me. Something popular with YA readers right now that doesn't involve royalty.*

A tinkling of chimes met her ears, and Matthew Talbot walked through the front door. She lingered for a moment, taking in his fashionable wool jacket and the tidy swoop of his chestnut hair. She'd never seen him in anything but clothing more suitable for working in the dirt than sitting behind an editorial desk.

Well, somebody's all cleaned up today. He hadn't been at work that morning, and Rodger hadn't mentioned why. But with the way he was dressed, it sure didn't seem like a last-minute emergency.

His hazel eyes met hers, and her stomach squeezed. *No, do not come over here. I do not feel like dealing with you today.*

But it was too late. He sauntered over to the YA section and gave her an affable grin. "Hey, Anna. What are you doing here? Shouldn't you be at the inn?"

She stared at him, internally cursing the cute dimple in his chin. "I should be asking you the same thing." She lifted her nose and continued to browse through the book spines on the shelf. "We missed you this morning. Rodger could have used the extra help tearing out that old milk tank."

He narrowed his eyes at her. "You missed me, huh?"

Anna fought the urge to roll her eyes. "No. That's not what I meant. Rodger—"

Matthew chuckled, causing the lines around his eyes to crinkle with mischief. "I know. It was a joke."

She took a breath, annoyed with herself. *Get a hold of yourself, Anna. We are coworkers, and we made an agreement to be civil.* "Right. I knew that."

She straightened her book bag, forcing her shoulders to relax. Her gaze caught on him, and she wondered what it would be like to run her fingers through the tousled waves of his hair. *Wait. Stop. Civil doesn't mean caressing the man!*

"I'm sorry if I left you all in a bind," he said, oblivious to her discomfort. "I didn't plan on missing work today. I had to run my mom to the hospital this morning."

"Oh! Is she alright?"

"Yeah, she's okay. A bruised hip from a fall, a sprained ankle from yoga."

"From yoga?"

"It's a long story." He glanced around the store and lowered his voice. "But we can blame Christine for the yoga incident." He smirked, clearly teasing her again. "By the time we were out of Emergency, Rodger said things were wrapping up for the day and to wait and come in tomorrow."

Anna's heart softened. She could be annoyed with Matthew all she wanted, but not his mom. She'd met Paula Talbot a few times through Madison and Marshal, and the woman had always been kind to her. "Well, I'm glad your mom will be okay. That's definitely a good reason to miss work."

"I'm glad it meets your approval." He lifted a brow, then followed her gaze to the bookshelf. "YA fairy tales? Is that what genre you write?"

"It's more like what my agent wants me to write." Anna gestured at the line of books helplessly. "I wrote *The Wicked Moon* for adults. Now, Clarissa wants me to change it to YA so publishers will be more interested. Apparently, fairies are in for teens right now."

"Hmm." Matthew nodded, appraising the books in front of them. "Well, she's right about that. You said *The Wicked Moon*, right? I think I remember your proposal, and it was definitely not a book for kids. There's a lot to consider when switching the intended audience. You wouldn't want to lose the heart of your story."

"That's exactly what I'm worried about." Anna stepped closer to him and pulled a canary-yellow paperback from the shelf. "She's not a princess like these heroines. And the book isn't all magic and stardust, there's some bad things that happened in Rowena's life that she has to overcome. She's lived in my head for years, and she's always been in her late twenties with adult problems. Now, I have to somehow make her a high school student, change her backstory, adjust the romance…"

"Why don't you write something new? Let *The Wicked Moon* sit for a bit. Wait for the right publisher to bite."

"I'm scared Clarissa isn't that patient." Anna returned the book to its spot, then twisted to face him. "I think she might drop me as an author if I don't do what she thinks is best. And I mean, she's a literary agent. She knows the business way better than I do."

Matthew rubbed his chin, looking at her intently. "Ah, but you are the author. You need to do what's right by your work. And if writing YA fairy tales isn't your passion, readers—and acquisitions editors—will be able to tell."

She pushed her glasses up her nose, her heart sinking. "Then what am I supposed to do?"

"Do you have any other projects you're working on?"

"I do. But it's not fantasy. It's a story about two estranged sisters who go on a hiking trip together to reconnect. Clarissa has no interest in women's fiction."

Matthew tilted his head. "That sounds promising. I know a few agents searching for stories like that. If you like, I could take a look at it."

"Oh, no." Anna took a step back, her chest tight. "It's nowhere near ready for an editor. I only have the first few chapters written, and I'm still tweaking the plot."

"Think of it more as a critique than an edit," Matthew replied. "Free of charge, of course. An outline and a chapter are a good start. If you have the premise ironed out and get a couple more chapters written, we could shine them up and you could shop them around."

"Oh, I don't know." Anna wasn't sure what to say. She gave him a sideways look, trying to figure out his angle. It was a nice offer, but what was in it for him?

"Well, think about it and let me know." He glanced around the store, his brows knit with confusion. "I was going to head over to the women's fiction section to show you a book I think you should read, but this store doesn't make any sense. Why is horror between romance and gluten-free cookbooks?"

Anna laughed and beckoned at him to follow her. "That's Christine's style, organized chaos. You should see her tea wall. She has the English breakfast with the herbal tisanes."

"Well, that's just blasphemous."

"Right? Though honestly, despite the disordered displays, Christine's wonderful. She's been nothing but supportive of my writing." Anna stopped in front of a floor-to-ceiling bookcase lined with titles about everything from religion, to gardening, to astrology, and finally, fiction books with scenic photos and joyful-looking women on the covers.

"That doesn't surprise me. She's Sophie's mom, after all." Matthew stood beside her, appraising the books.

"That's right. Sophie dates your brother."

"Yup. I grew up with Soph. Though she's Marshal and Madi's age, so I don't know her as well as they do." He stepped forward, his elbow brushing Anna's as he went, and picked a title from the highest shelf. "Here, this one's a new release. I read it last month, and it's about two sisters who are rival athletes. Their family goes on a trip to Italy and they get lost in Venice together." He handed her the book, and his eyes crinkled with humour. "Touching and hilarious."

Anna took it from him, gazing at the bright blue water of the canal on the cover. "You read women's fiction novels?"

He gave her a sheepish grin. "I read everything. Science fiction is my favourite, but I'll let you in on a secret, if you promise you won't tell Sophie or Madison."

"What?"

"I read a few of my sister's romance novels growing up. Cheesy, yes. But I dig heartwarming. There was this one by Celia Saint James I probably read a dozen times." He furrowed his brows. "I can't remember what it was called. But it had a purple cover with a couple—" His eyes widened as if he'd caught himself divulging his deepest secret, and he pointed a finger at her. "Marshal can never find out. Ever."

Anna giggled and tucked the book under her arm. "Your promise is safe with me. Book nerds have to stick together."

"True. Especially book nerds who were both let go by the same press."

Her throat tightened. For a moment, she'd almost forgotten that he was the guy who'd pulled the rug from under her publishing dreams. And he wanted to look at her manuscript? *No way.*

Laura came around the corner of the bookshelf behind him, holding a cardboard box filled with paperbacks. "Oh, hi, Anna!" She paused, looking at Matthew. "Hi there, I'm Laura."

"Hey, I'm Matthew. I'd offer to shake your hand, but yours are full. Need help with that box?"

"Oh, I was about to set this down." She nodded in his direction, causing her blonde bangs to fall in her face. "These ones go on that shelf right behind you."

She let him take the box, then he set it down on the hardwood chair at the end of the shelf. "Are they okay here?"

"You bet! Thank you." Laura pushed the stray locks from her forehead, then turned to Anna. "Hey, have you decided if you're coming to the Book Club meeting on Friday?"

Anna cringed, remembering that she'd meant to avoid the clerk until after Friday. *Right. The book club.* "Umm, you know, I'm not sure."

"Book club meeting?" Matthew asked. "Here, at the store?"

"Yep," Laura replied. "We start at seven o'clock sharp. Like I told Anna the other day, we're deciding on the Christmas book for this year. New people are always welcome, but only if you don't suggest any boring classics."

"What about Silent Night by John Glover?"

Laura crossed her arms and quirked a brow. "I haven't heard of that, but it sounds bland."

"It's horror."

"You're in. And don't forget that recommendation."

Matthew pumped his arm. "Awesome."

Anna shook her head, trying to hide a laugh. *Who'd have thought Mr. Pompous Editor was such a dork?*

Laura turned her pleading gaze to Anna. "You're going to come too, right? I promise, there's no pressure to share your work. Just a bunch of readers chatting about books."

"A bunch of book nerds, as you said," Matthew agreed. "It'll be fun."

Anna bit the inside of her lip, folding under Laura's imploring gaze. "Okay. Fridays are my night off from the kitchen anyways." *A night I was planning to spend writing.* But she didn't need to tell them that.

"Perfect!" Laura clasped her hands together. "I'm so glad. Okay, I gotta get these books shelved. I'll see both of you on Friday."

"You bet," Matthew replied. "Looking forward to whatever Christmassy reads you two come up with."

Anna's phone vibrated in her pocket, and she shifted the book to her other arm so she could pull it out.

An alarm lit up her screen, letting her know it was almost time for her kitchen shift.

"Shoot. It's almost time for work." She put her phone away, then waved the book in their direction. "I better pay for this and get going. Thanks for the recommendation, Matthew."

"Hope it helps."

"Me too." She said good-bye to Laura, then made her way to the front of the store to pay for the book. She caught the sound of Matthew and Laura's laughter, and her throat tightened. Were they flirting? *That's none of your business, Anna.* But still, a tiny part of her cringed at the thought. She could hardly blame Matthew if he was. The blond clerk was not only pretty, but charming and funny too. *Nothing like me.*

She clenched her jaw. *I've got to stop wallowing! I'm not interested in him like that, anyways. Right?* Forcing her gaze to the tea behind the counter, she set down the hardcover and rang the bell, hoping Christine would hear it from the back room.

The price on the book stood out on a bright red sticker. Anna winced, realizing it wasn't even in the genre she'd needed for *The Wicked Moon*.

But she couldn't bring herself to put it back, and Matthew's words of encouragement came to her mind. Begrudgingly, she had to admit he was right. Her heart and mind needed something more than her rejected fae story. She welcomed the thought of something fresh and new to dive into.

Maybe tonight I'll work on my mountain story, after I tear apart chapter seven of The Wicked Moon. Her mind began to wander into the woods, pulling memories of hiking trips in the Rockies her mother had forced her to go on as a child. Pouring rain and slick rocks, the fear of grizzly bears hanging above her head—*I can use this. One of the sisters definitely hates the idea of spending time in the wilderness. Now, how can I get her to the point of a weeks-long hiking trip with her estranged sister?*

Matthew's hearty laughter sounded behind her again, but she fought the jealousy rising within her and resisted turning around to look at him. *Who'd have thought he'd be so helpful? And funny? A man who reads romance books...* She pressed her lips together to hide her smile.

She rang the bell again, in case Christine didn't hear it the first time. Matthew's offer to help with her new story was tempting. But what if he didn't like it? What if he told her the exact words she'd been dreading to hear, the very thing her mother had been pressing on her for months—that she wasn't cut out to be an author?

No, better not take the chance to find out. Especially from Mr. Pompous Editor. Or is it Mr. Book-nerd Editor now? She shook her head. Either way, there was no way she could let him see her story.

Chapter Nine

Matthew stepped away from Rodger's pickup truck, listening to his mother's voice on the other end of the phone. She'd called during his break, right after he and Rodger had finished loading some old scrap metal and broken tools into the truck box.

"Your father had an interesting lunch with Don the other day…"

Anna came striding up the path from the inn, her arms loaded with cardboard coffee cups and a plastic container that probably contained some sort of sweet treat. Katie had called Rodger's cell and said Sophie had snacks lined up for them, and Anna had gone to get them. Now, she approached Rodger and Violet, who had gathered around the truck, and handed them each a cup.

Her cheeks were flushed pink in the cool weather, and her hair stuck out at odd angles beneath her knit hat.

How does she manage to make a down vest, work jeans, and messy hair look so good?

She'd been friendly to him all morning, helping him sweep out the last of the dust in the loft and chatting animatedly about books and movies. Their talk in the bookshop yesterday seemed to have melted her icy exterior. He'd enjoyed working next to her, captivated by her quick wit and heartfelt explanation of her book characters' romantic sub-plot.

His mother continued, "…and he really thinks it would be a good opportunity for you…"

Anna set the plastic container on the lowered tailgate, then laughed at something Rodger said. Matthew gazed at her, admiring the curve of her lips and the way the tips of her hair barely brushed her slim shoulders when she lifted her chin—

Paula's voice grounded him back to his phone. "What do you think? We're having dinner with him tomorrow night at Hunters' Steakhouse," she said. "If you'd like to join us, we could introduce you. See if you'd be a good fit."

Matthew turned to concentrate on the conversation. "Er—sorry. Dinner with who?"

Paula let out an exasperated sigh. "Don Willingham. The manager of the public library."

"Um, okay—"

"Were you listening to me at all, dear? He has an opening for a librarian position."

A librarian job? Why would she think I'd be interested in that? He scratched the back of his neck with his free hand. "Thanks Mom, but that's not really what I'm looking for. Besides, I have plans tomorrow night."

"Well, it would be a proper job, at least." She paused. "You have plans? What kind of plans?"

"Just a book club thing with a friend," he replied. With the way things had been going, he could call Anna a friend, right?

As if on cue, Anna laughed again and he twisted toward her. She caught his eye, then held up a coffee cup and pointed at it, signaling it was for him. His chest warmed, and he gave her a wave of acknowledgement.

"Look Mom, I have to go. But I'll call you later, okay?"

"Alright," Paula relented. "But if you change your mind about tomorrow—"

"I won't. But we can chat this weekend about what kind of job I'm qualified for, okay?"

"Okay," she agreed. "Oh, and I have an old water trough here for you to haul to the inn next week. I think it'd make a nice planter to put next to the barn door."

"Sounds good. We'll load it into Marshal's truck after Sunday dinner."

They said goodbye, and he tucked his phone into the back pocket of his jeans and made his way to the group at the truck.

Anna handed him a coffee, then jerked her elbow in the direction of the plastic container on the tailgate. Violet stood in front of it, appraising the contents, and Anna grinned. "Sophie's pumpkin muffins with cream cheese icing. You better grab one before Violet clears them out."

Matthew chuckled and took the cup from her. "Coffee's fine for now. I'll let Violet have her pick of the sweets first."

Violet darted her gaze to Anna and cocked her head. "Hey, I'm a growing teen. I need calories."

Rodger gestured toward the barn. "Yep, you better load up for the job I've got for you next. You'll need the energy."

Her face fell and she gave him a wary look. "Does it have anything to do with scraping ancient manure again?"

"Not this time," Rodger replied. "There's a couple old saddles and other odds and ends in the back room that were left there years ago. I don't know what shape they're in, but if you haul them to the stable and clean them up, we can see if one might be suitable for that new horse of yours."

Violet's eyes lit up. She grabbed a muffin, then practically skipped to Rodger's side. "Deal!"

"A new horse?" Anna asked, her eyes almost as bright as Violet's. "That's exciting, Violet!"

"Thanks," she replied, beaming. "I joined the 4-H horse club. Dusty's a buckskin—the prettiest horse I've ever seen. I can't wait to show him off to my friends!"

Matthew took a sip of his coffee and nodded. "You're one lucky kid. Madison begged our parents for a horse when she was your age. That was one thing Dad refused to indulge her in."

Rodger took a big swig from his cup, then tossed it into box of the truck. "Alright, kiddo. Shall we go check out those saddles?"

"Yes!"

"You two finish up your coffees before heading in," Rodger said. "All that old twine in the loft needs to come out next."

"Sounds good," Matthew replied, tipping his cup toward them. With a wave, they were off, Violet leading the way with an excited bounce in her step.

Before he could turn to Anna to thank her for retrieving the treats, Matthew's phone vibrated in his pocket. He took it out, and a text from his mom blinked on the screen.

Here's Don's email address, in case you change your mind and would like to send him your resume.

Matthew bit back a sigh and shook his head, then jammed his phone in his pocket.

"Somebody pestering you?" Anna leaned her hip on the side of the truck, cradling her coffee with both hands.

Matthew snorted. "Sort of. How could you tell?"

She shrugged. "The scowl on your face gave it away."

"That obvious, huh?" He shook his head. "It was just my mom, trying to set me up with a librarian job."

Anna furrowed her brows and pushed her glasses up her nose. "A librarian job?"

"Yeah. Not exactly in my wheelhouse," he replied. "She doesn't really understand the book industry."

Anna gave him an understanding nod. "Neither does my family. If you don't mind me asking, what are your career plans now that Raven Stone's gone under?"

"I'm not sure." Matthew sipped his coffee, taking in the bitter flavour. "I don't want to move far away again for an in-house job. I've been trying to scrounge up some freelancing gigs, but it's not going well. I don't how to find clients."

"Surely you have some contacts who could help you out?"

He shook his head. "Most of my university buddies work for media outlets or big-name publishers."

"What about your past clients through Raven Stone?"

He shifted self-consciously under her pretty gaze. "I don't know if that's a good idea, or if I'm even allowed to contact them."

"I don't see why not. The company doesn't even exist anymore, there shouldn't be any conflicts," Anna replied. "I'm in touch with a few of the other authors who lost their contracts. Some are considering self-publishing, and others are shopping their manuscripts around again. Either way, I bet a few of them would be interested in paying for some editing."

Matthew raised his brows. "And how do you think they'd respond to me, the editor who cut their contracts? The same way you did at first?"

She giggled and gave him a sideways look, causing his chest to tighten. "I could vouch for you and pass your website along to them. That way, it'd be coming from somebody they trust."

Matthew rubbed his chin with his free hand, mulling over her words. She had a point. It would be a good way to kick start his business, and he could give past Raven Stone authors a discount as an olive branch. He could help them get their books back on track while getting his freelance business rolling at the same time.

"That's a *really* good idea. Thank you. The only thing is, my website is a mess. Why don't I fix it first?

Then I'll send it your way."

Anna gestured with her cup in a cheers motion. "That sounds good. Let me know when it's ready."

Matthew raised his cup to hers, and their fingers brushed for a second, sending a tingle through his hand. He lowered it, taking in the way she darted her gaze from him and tugged at the zipper of her vest with her dainty fingers. He wondered what it would feel like to hold her hand—

"So, are we still on for the book club meeting tomorrow at seven?" she asked.

He blinked, suddenly remembering their date tomorrow. Or was it date? Should he ask her if it was? *No! I have to stop acting like an awkward teenager.* "Umm, yeah. Sure. I'll meet you there." He paused, trying to ground himself. "Looking forward to it, and I'm ready to battle for my choice of Christmas book."

Anna giggled, then tossed her empty cup into the box of Rodger's truck with the rest of the garbage destined for the dump. "Well, I guess we should get back to it. What did Rodger say earlier? That barn isn't going to clean itself?"

"Something like that," Matthew agreed. He drank his last mouthful of coffee while she put the lid on the plastic container and set it inside the truck cab, then they started toward the entrance of the barn.

Who would have thought an ex-author from Raven Stone would be willing to suggest my editing services to her peers? They reached the doorway, and he hesitated and touched her elbow. "Hey, Anna?"

"Yes?"

"Have you thought any more about having me look at your new manuscript?" he asked. "I could do an assessment of your fairy book too, if you're interested. Free of charge, of course."

Anna chewed her bottom lip. "I don't know. I feel guilty taking advantage of you. I know how much work editing is, and it isn't cheap."

"You wouldn't be taking advantage of me," he replied. "If it would make you feel better, you could write me a testimonial to use for my website. If you like my work, that is." He hesitated. "No pressure, though. I only want to help."

"I'll think about."

"Alright. Let's go tackle that loft." He grabbed the

rusty handle, then slid open the barn door.

"Thanks." She dipped her head, then stepped inside.

Matthew gazed after her, a hint of worry forming in the back of his head. *This girl.* He'd only meant to smooth things out between them. To make her not hate him anymore, and to help her with her writing. But the ache that formed inside him every time he saw her... He shrugged it off and closed the door behind him. *We're both adults. It's not as if anything more than friendship has happened between us.*

And nothing more would. Right?

Chapter Ten

Matthew took a step back and admired the greenhouse wall before him. The polycarbonate sheets were solidly in place, and after finishing the south-facing wall, all they had left was to build the raised beds Marshal had plotted out. Well, that and have the electrician come out and wire everything in. But with sun in the forecast, things were looking up for Marshal. Matthew thought of all the spindly seedlings sitting in Marshal's living room under grow lights. *Maybe we'll get them moved in here yet.*

The setting sun cast a warm glow through the translucent walls. Matthew glanced at his watch, then gave the sealant gun in his hand a slight toss, satisfied with his work. *See? I'm no Marshal, but I'm not completely useless at this stuff.*

Now, he had to head to the house and get ready for the book club meeting at Christine's shop. He'd been looking forward to it all day, thinking about the other afternoon at the shop with Anna—when he'd finally thawed her ice queen demeanor. And since then, they'd only been growing closer at work. With her quirky humour and the passionate way she explained the different types of fae creatures in her book, she'd made the mornings filled with scraping grime from the barn floors, cleaning moldy hay from the loft, and pressure washing the walls downright enjoyable.

He'd been thinking about her so much that even Marshal had teased him about having his head in the clouds the evening before. They'd been playing *Fallout*, and Matthew had zoned out and allowed a ghoul to walk right into their compound.

And he wasn't even that sorry about it. Thoughts of Anna's deep brown eyes and musical laughter were a lot nicer than the dystopian nightmare of his and Marshal's video game. Now, he couldn't wait to see her outside of work. In her element, the bookstore.

He made his way outside to Marshal's truck, which was parked next to the structure. More polycarbonate sheets lay stacked in the back with their ends hanging over the lowered tailgate. Marshal stood next to the sheets with a pencil in mouth, going over the blueprint spread out on top of the pile.

He looked up at Matthew's approach and took the pencil from between his teeth. "Hey, got that wall finished?"

"You bet." Matthew opened the passenger door and placed the sealant gun in the box of supplies on the passenger seat. "I got the panels taped and sealed. Even if it rains tonight, they should be fine."

"Huh. Good work. Guess you have a little handyman in you after all." Marshal pointed the pencil in his direction. "The forecast looks okay for a few days. Let's try to get the rest of these up this weekend before the rain hits again."

"Sure thing." Matthew reached across the box to the cooler sitting next to it and grabbed a bottle of water. "We're moving faster than expected at the inn, so Rodger told us to take the weekend off there anyways." He held up the bottle. "Want one?"

"Sure, thanks." Marshal tucked the pencil in the front pocket of his flannel shirt, making Matthew grin. He reminded Matthew of their old man, not only in looks but in mannerisms too. Bill always had a pen or pencil sticking out of his front pocket, whether at his clinic or working on a project around home.

Matthew grabbed a second bottle, then slammed the lid of the cooler shut. He wandered over to Marshal and handed him the water.

Marshal took it and untwisted the lid. "What are you doing for supper tonight? Me and Soph are going to catch a bite at Last Call with Dylan and Madi. Do you want to come?"

"And be the fifth wheel?" Matthew leaned his elbows on the truck box and shook his head. "Nah. Besides, I have a book club meeting tonight at seven."

Marshal squinted at him over the bottle as he took a drink. "A book club meeting? At Christine's?"

Matthew nodded. "Yeah. I went in there the other day after I brought Mom to the hospital. The clerk, I think her name's Laura, invited me."

"Ah, a girl. I figured there was more to it than books," Marshal replied. "There's no way I could sit in that store all night with those clucking hens."

Matthew raised his brows. "Clucking hens?"

"They'll be fighting over beach romances or those mysteries about old ladies who like to knit and have ten cats," Marshal said with a grin. "Or Christine will have you reading some book on mystical aliens."

"You sure know a lot about cozy mysteries," Matthew replied. "Got some Agatha Christie novels hiding around the house?"

"No, but I can talk to Sophie if you're looking."

Matthew chuckled and took a drink of his water. "Well, it can't be that bad. I miss being around people who love books. And Anna's going—"

"Anna?" Marshal cocked his head. "Sophie's assistant from the inn? She mentioned you two were both messed over by Raven Stone. Are you two—nah. Never mind. It's none of my business."

"You're right. It's not. But no, we're just friends." Matthew averted his gaze. "Hey, have you talked to Mom?"

"Yeah." Marshal wandered to the driver's side of

the truck and opened the door, then tossed his now-empty water bottle into the garbage bag behind the seat. "You know her, she's tough. I'm sure she's driving Dad crazy, galloping around the house on those crutches with her sprained ankle. She seemed pretty excited about those milk cans."

Matthew bobbed his head. He'd meant to give her a call. But after her meddling about job prospects, he'd been hesitant to open that can of worms again.

Marshal cleared this throat. "She's worried about you, you know."

"I know."

Marshal closed the truck door, then caught Matthew's eye. "She only wants the family closer together. She was sad when you moved to Toronto, and when Madison—well, you know. When that scumbag ex-husband of hers got between her and the family."

Matthew grimaced. "I'm trying, Marsh. I've been going to family suppers and making a point to be around now that I'm home."

Marshal nodded and walked around the truck to join his side. "I know. I think she's scared you're going to get a new job in New York or something like that.

It was just Mom, Dad, and me around here for years. She's happy to have all her kids home again."

"I'm not leaving Canada, that's for sure," Matthew replied. "But I don't know where things will take me yet. I have some ideas to scrounge up freelance work. I made a listing on Editors Canada, but I need to get my website and social media going. If I could build my own business, I could work from home. I wouldn't have to move again."

A pop song rang out from Marshal's direction, and he pulled out his phone from the pocket of his vest.

"Taylor Swift?" Mathew gave him an incredulous look. "And you were making fun of me about cozy mystery books?"

Marshal furrowed his brows. "It's Sophie, and she put the song on here."

"Sure, she did."

Marshal jerked his head toward the house. "I've got to take this. Get going inside, I'll catch up later."

Matthew shrugged, then sauntered toward the old farmhouse, his water still in hand. *Maybe Anna's right about those authors. So what if some have less than friendly feelings toward me? Some might not. And I could prove to them that I want to help them.*

And then, he could stick around Cedar Lake. He had to admit, despite Marshal being a pain lately, he liked living with his brother and being involved with his family again. Even his hometown had been growing on him. The quiet roads. The friendly, familiar faces. Anna Simone.

We'll see how this freelancing thing goes. He knew it wouldn't be easy, but he could still keep an eye out for a job with a publisher on the west coast. He could keep both options open, which would only further his chances at staying somewhat closer to home.

Anna ran her flat iron over the lock of hair in her fingers, admiring her smooth tresses in the mirror above her dresser. Monty lay on the yellow comforter on her bed, watching her with his head nestled between his paws. They'd just returned home from their Friday afternoon romp around the lake, and now the affable dog was ready for his regular nap.

Her laptop sat open on the corner of the dresser, her sister's face filling the screen.

"So, let me get this straight," Kelsey said, her usual wine glass in hand. "Now Matthew is actually pretty cool, and he offered to look over the first few chapters of your new manuscript? Why on earth didn't you take him up on it?"

Anna frowned and sectioned a new portion of hair with her fingers. "His offer is still there, I think. But I didn't know how to bring it up again, you know?" She clamped the tool on her wavy tress and slid it over her hair.

"No, I don't know." Kelsey took a sip from her glass. "He's a professional editor. Why wouldn't you want his help?"

"Kels, you're not a writer. You don't get it." Anna placed the straightener on top of her dresser and whirled to face the laptop. "He rejected *The Wicked Moon* based only on its proposal. He didn't even read it."

"Exactly," Kelsey replied. "So he has no idea how good you are. Didn't your agent write the proposal, not you?"

"Yes, but that's beside the point. The premise of the story is mine." Anna sighed and drummed her fingers on the dresser's surface. "He can be so intimidating. He's all dimples and suave hair and broad shoulders—and an editor on top of it all."

"Hold on." Kelsey held up her free hand. A slow grin crept across her face. "Anna, do you have a thing for Mr. Pompous Editor?"

Anna huffed so loudly that even Monty raised his head. She walked to the bed and stroked his neck. Matthew had been extra kind to her the last few days at work. He'd listened patiently about her pains with *The Wicked Moon*, and even discussed his issues with finding work and seemed to respect her advice. He'd made her feel important, like her opinion and experience mattered. He'd even brought her tea from Valley Roast this morning—a matcha latté, exactly like she had ordered when they were in town together on Tuesday.

Come off it, Anna. He brought Rodger and Violet drinks too. It doesn't mean anything.

"Come on, Kels. He's this successful guy, making a career in the book world. And he didn't like my work." She returned to the dresser and peered at her sister. "I know I need to get over it, especially if I want to be an author. Critique is part of the game. But I didn't think I'd have to face one of those critics in person."

She thought of his dimpled smile and her stomach fluttered. *And I didn't think he'd be so charming, either.*

Kelsey gave her a sympathetic look. "You're right, I haven't been there. But I can imagine how rough it is. When that professor tore me down in vet school—well, what I mean to say is, we all face rejection. But you shouldn't quit." She paused. "Maybe you met Matthew for a reason. You know, some sort of life lesson."

Anna rolled her eyes and leaned closer to the screen. "Now you're sounding like Christine."

"Christine? The owner of the bookshop?"

"Oh yeah, she's super into spiritual stuff. Tarot cards. Gemstones. You name it."

"Maybe she'll have a message from the unknown for you tonight." Kelsey wiggled the fingers of her free hand in Anna's direction. "About a handsome editor and a manuscript that could use a professional gaze." She widened her eyes. "And a lost author who could use a little *gazing upon* by said editor herself—"

Anna snorted and shook her head. "I gotta go." She checked the clock in the corner of the computer screen. "I have to be there in fifteen minutes."

"Okay," Kelsey replied. "Have fun. And let me know tomorrow if anything happens between you and Mr. Not-so-pompous Editor—"

"Kelsey," Anna warned her.

"One last thing, Annie."

"What?"

Kelsey tugged at a lock of hair behind her ear. "You missed a spot. Right here. Left side."

Anna groaned and pawed at her hair, finding the stray curl. "Thank you. Good night."

"Night."

The computer went dark. Anna closed it, then picked up her flat iron and fixed her hair, swiped on a coat of mascara, and double-checked that the olive-green blouse she wore had no dog hair stuck to it. She glanced over her shoulder at Monty. "What do you think, buddy? Does this shirt compliment my skin tone?"

Monty cocked his head in silent approval, wagging his tail across the blanket.

Anna picked up a microfibre cloth from the ceramic tray on her dresser. She pulled off her glasses and cleaned the lenses, then slid them back on and looked at herself in the mirror. *Why did I even bother straightening my hair?*

It's just a book club meeting. I could show up in a hoodie and a messy bun, and nobody would bat an eye.

But maybe she wanted somebody to bat an eye. Maybe she wanted to seem confident and put together, especially in front of Matthew. And what could be wrong with that? She could make a connection with him. As an author, of course. *Networking, that's what they call it, right?*

She went to her bed and gave Monty a final pat on the head, promising she wouldn't be too long, then made her way to the door and grabbed her wool jacket off the hook. After slipping it on, she picked up her purse and left for the bookstore.

Once outside, the white lights Christine had strung across the storefront window caught her eye. With the burgundy leaves on the trees that framed the doorway, it looked like a magical portal into a fantasy land. In a way, that's exactly what Steeped in Books was.

Anna ducked her head against the cold breeze and hustled across the street, searching for Matthew's car. She didn't see the red Toyota in any of the parking spots yet, so she paused in front of the shop's door, wondering if she should wait for him outside.

He'd told her that morning he would meet her there. Did that mean he wanted to go in with her? Or that he would meet her inside?

Before she could make up her mind, a familiar deep voice came from behind her.

"Anna Simone? What are you doing here?"

Anna spun around, her heart in her throat. Sure enough, Jace Cook stood staring at her as if she'd sprouted wings right in front of him. With his shoulder-length blond hair waving in the breeze and his hands in the pockets of his leather bomber, he looked as though he'd stepped out of the pages of a fashion magazine.

Anna swallowed and slid her gaze to the woman next to him, who grabbed his hand and gave Anna a bored look. She pushed her silky blond hair from her face, and Anna recognized her as Jillian—the ex-now-current girlfriend Jace had broken up with Anna for.

"Uh, hey." Heat crept up Anna's neck. She loosened her scarf with trembling fingers. "I'm here for the book club meeting. You?"

"That's why we're here too," Jace replied. "Jilly

Bean wanted to check it out, didn't you?" He gave the woman an adoring smile. "There's no bookstore in Rocky Ridge," he said, referring to the neighbouring town where he lived. "This is the closest one."

Jillian gave the front window a look of disdain. "It's… cute. Quaint, I guess. I hope they actually carry some literature I'm interested in and not only genre fiction."

Jilly Bean? Anna glanced at Jillian. *What's wrong with genre fiction? Romance, fantasy, mysteries—readers love them.* "Oh. Cool. This is a great store. Christine carries all kinds of books. I'm sure she'll have something you like."

"Yeah." Jace shifted, looking her up and down with his piercing blue eyes. "Speaking of books and genre fiction, I heard you lost your contract for your little fairy book. Tough deal."

Little fairy book? The heat in Anna's face swept to her ears. When they were together, he'd seemed excited for her when she'd landed the deal. Apparently, his tastes had changed. "Um, my agent is shopping it around again—"

Jillian leaned against Jace's shoulder and let out a loud sigh. "Are you here by yourself? Should we go inside?"

Anna took a step back, her tongue stuck in her throat.

She clenched her jaw, struggling to think of something to say. Her pulse raced with the urge to spin on her heel and escape the situation. To skip the meeting altogether and go home to work on her manuscript with a soothing cup of tea and Monty by her side.

"Hey, Anna." Matthew's friendly voice interrupted her panicked thoughts. He hit the button on his keys to lock his car, then joined them at the door. She looked him up and down, her cheeks growing even warmer as she took in his black wool jacket and his handsomely tousled hair.

He came to stand beside her and shot Jace a friendly, yet firm, smile. "Hey, I'm Matthew. A friend of Anna's."

Anna continued to stare at him, grateful he'd arrived when he did. "Hi." She gestured toward Jace. "This is Jace." She paused, the words *my ex-boyfriend* stuck in her mouth. "And Jillian. Anyways, we should head inside. I think the meeting is starting soon."

"Sounds good to me." Matthew nodded at the couple and stepped by them to open the door.

"Uh, thanks, man." Jace led his girlfriend into the shop without a backwards glance.

Matthew raised a brow. "They friends of yours?"

Anna shook her head. "Not really. It's a long story. But I dated Jace, once upon a time. And he dumped me for her."

"Ouch." Matthew gave her a sympathetic look. "Well, we'll make sure to sit far away from them." He leaned toward her and lowered his voice. "Are their names really Jace and Jillian? That's weird."

The woodsy smell of his aftershave went straight to Anna's head, and her heart drummed against her ribs. She giggled, then wrinkled her nose. "He calls her *Jilly Bean*."

"You've got to be kidding me." Matthew pressed his lips together as if he were holding back a laugh, then gestured for her to step inside while he held the door.

Anna stepped by him and entered the shop. Her jacket brushed against his as she went, sending a warm quiver up her arm. *Why am I being like this? Behaving like a teenage girl on her first date!* As far as she knew, this wasn't a date. Or was it? *Stop it, Anna. Be normal.* She took a deep breath to steady her nerves.

Matthew let the door close behind them. She gazed around the store, taking in the twinkle lights that ran along the bookcases and the snack table piled with treats and a coffee urn with paper cups next to it. Jace and his girlfriend had chosen seats in the front row of chairs in the middle of the room.

It's going to be okay. We can sit here, listen to the discussion, and leave before snack and chat time. I won't have to say another word to those two.

As she picked a spot for her and Matthew in the back row, Jace turned his head and gave her a quick glance. Matthew held out a chair for her to sit in, and her chest squeezed.

She thought back to Kelsey's words earlier, *do you have a thing for Mr. Pompous Editor?* As much as she hated to admit it, maybe her sister was on to something.

CHAPTER ELEVEN

Matthew leaned back in his seat, trying to hold in a laugh. The centre of the store had been cleared; the book-laden tables pushed aside to make room for the three rows of chairs for the book club. He and Anna had sat in the back, and only about a dozen other people were there—mostly women, a few who Matthew recognized from around town.

The clerk he'd met the other day, Laura, stood at the front counter with her arms crossed and an annoyed look on her face. A purple banner that read *The Page Turners* in white script had been strung across the baskets of tea on the wall behind her.

"Joanne, we are not reading *the Nutcracker and the Mouse King*. I know it's a classic, but I think I'm not alone when I say we'd rather read something, well, fun. And maybe written in a language we can understand."

A middle-aged woman in the second row with bright mahogany hair crossed her arms and let out a loud huff. "Do you think the members here can't read English, Laura?"

An elderly lady sitting a few chairs over from her twisted in her seat. The chain on her cat-eye glasses caught on the brooch on her knitted sweater. "The language is a bit dated, Joanne. Even for me."

"What do you suggest then, Lizzie?" Joanne shot back. "One of those bodice rippers I saw in your knitting bag last week at craft night?"

Lizzie snapped her mouth shut, giving Joanne one of the sharpest glares Matthew had ever seen.

Anna shifted next to him. When he looked at her, she caught his eye and gave him an amused shrug.

As Laura and Joanne continued to bicker, Jace stared into space from his seat at the front, as if ignoring the situation completely. Beside him, Jillian tapped at her phone screen. Matthew had a feeling they wouldn't be back, which was fine with him.

What had Anna seen in that guy, anyways? He doesn't seem like her type—not that I would know.

It's probably not the editor who tore her book to shreds either. He looked at her from the corner of his eye, taking in the soft lines of her dainty chin and wondering what Jace had said to her outside before the meeting. From the look of her ashen face, it hadn't been nice.

Christine's serene voice floated over the group, bringing his attention to the front of the room. She made her way behind the front desk, her gauzy dress wrapped around her like an ethereal mummy, and rummaged in the drawer beneath the till. "I think what we need is something to calm our nerves."

She pulled out a small bottle, unscrewed the lid, and proceeded to add a few drops from it to the Buddha-shaped oil diffuser on the edge of the counter. She hit the button on Buddha's leg and a few seconds later, steam began to waft from his head. A heavy, floral scent filled the room.

Matthew leaned his head toward Anna. "What is that? It smells like my grandmother's living room."

Anna pursed her lips. "Lavender, I think? I recognize it from when the Blooming Box brought in lavender bouquets for a wedding last summer. My apartment smelled like this for weeks."

"The pain of living above a flower shop."

"I actually quite liked it."

Matthew gave her a sly look. "You'll be a wonderful grandma one day."

Anna lifted her chin. "Not all grandmas are the same. Besides, I happen to like quilts and tea and floral scents."

Of course she does. I bet her apartment is filled with lace doilies and dried flowers. He envisioned her curled up in an old armchair with her laptop and a steaming mug, her brows knit together in that cute look of concentration he recognized from work. The cold autumn rain pounding outside her window, with her dog sleeping on the rug at her feet. His lips twitched with a smile at the thought.

She was the complete opposite of Brittany, who loved to shop and stay out all night at clubs with her friends. Something Matthew had once enjoyed, but it had slowly lost its charm. By the end of their relationship, Brittany had complained loudly about him wanting to stay home. *What's so wrong with a night in, for once?* Playing board games with friends appealed to him much more than sitting at a table in a club, unable to hear his friends speak over the booming beat of dance music.

And staying in with Anna, reading next to her on the couch as she tapped away at her keyboard, her body leaning closer to him as she reached for her tea—

"What do you two think? Anna? Matthew?" Laura's voice jerked him back to attention. She stood next to the lavender-spewing Buddha, looking at them expectantly. "What kind of Christmas book do you want to read?"

"Oh, I don't know." Anna waved her hands toward the ladies seated in front of them. "I'm fine with whatever. They can decide."

"Matthew? You had an interesting idea the other day, a holiday horror novel."

He nodded. "That's right. *Silent Night* by John Glover. Tagline, can Jimmy escape the haunted workshop before he gets sleighed?"

Anna covered her mouth and snorted a laugh, but Laura was the only other person who chuckled.

Tough crowd.

"I am not reading horror." Joanne crossed her arms. "There is no way I'll even crack the spine of something like that."

The woman behind Joanne raised her hand in the air. "What about one of those Christmas-themed sweet romances? You know, a nice Nora Roberts or Debbie Macomber book? There are lots to choose from."

Christine leaned her elbows on the front desk, allowing the steam from the diffuser to waft above her head. "We had a shipment of books like that come in the other day. They're always a hit this time of year."

Before Joanne could object, Laura stepped forward. "That is a great idea, Sue. Everybody in favour?"

Matthew raised his hand along with Anna, who nudged him in the ribs playfully. "Romance, of course. Your favourite."

His stomach tightened. *Romance?* "My—what?"

Anna's grin widened. "Maybe you can suggest one of your favourite Celia Saint James novels?"

He stifled a laugh, then lowered his voice. "I thought I told you not to tell anybody."

"It's just us," she replied innocently, batting her long lashes at him.

He swallowed, then lifted his brow in amusement. "And a room filled with women who probably know my parents."

Joanne looked around at all the raised arms, then reluctantly raised hers too. "I guess it's better than horror."

Laura clapped her hands together. "Perfect. I'll send a list of choices and a survey in our Monday email. Please have your answers to me by Wednesday."

After a note about the upcoming Christmas party and an invitation for everybody to stay for snacks, Laura adjourned the meeting and closed the open notebook on the counter.

Right as Matthew was about to get to his feet and offer a hand to Anna, Christine bustled around the front desk with a wicker basket in her hands. "Before you all go for coffee, I have one more thing. We have four new Page Turners here tonight, and I wanted to give them a warm welcome." She beckoned for Jace and Jillian to join her at the front, then waved at Matthew and Anna.

Jace and Jillian exchanged horrified glances, not moving from their spots.

"Oh, no." Anna raised her palms in front of her. "I'm okay right here. Thanks, Christine."

Christine's face fell, and she dug a purple metallic button from the basket and held it up. "Official Page Turner" was emblazoned across it with an open book beneath the title. "I have these pins for new members—don't you want one?"

Lizzie grabbed her tote bag from beneath her chair and held it up for them to see. The same button was pinned to the side of it. "All members get one. You want to join us, don't you?"

"Yeah." Sue cranked her neck to join in. "Don't you want to be an official Page Turner?"

They didn't respond, and Matthew cringed. *Aww, come one. Somebody has to humour her*. He pushed back his chair and got to his feet. Anna's eyes grew wide. He gave her a sheepish shrug, then raised his voice. "I don't know about these other three, but I'd love a button, Christine."

Christine beamed at him as he made his way to the front desk. The smell of lavender grew stronger, and she pinned the button on his sweater as if it were a medal. She patted his chest and the corners of her bright green eyes crinkled. "There you go. Now you're an official Page Turner. Be sure to leave your email address with Laura before you go."

"I'm honoured." Matthew gave her a little bow, and the other members giggled in their seats.

"Oh, alright. Christine, I'd love one too." Anna stood from her chair and joined them at the counter. Matthew held his palm out to her for a high-five. She rolled her eyes at him, but slapped his hand anyways.

Ha! Who knew I could be such a good influence?

Christine pinned the button to Anna's blouse, then stared expectantly at Jace and Jillian, who both looked like they wanted to be anywhere other than that bookstore. "It's okay if you're shy. You don't have to come up," she said kindly. She walked over to them and handed them each a pin. "You're welcome here any time."

Jillian gave her a tight smile, and then everyone else got to their feet and started to make their way to the coffee and snack table. Jace and Jillian grabbed their coats and slipped out the door.

Good. Hopefully they won't be back.

He shifted his gaze to Anna and tapped the pin on his sweater. "So? How does it feel to be an official Page Turner?"

"Magical," she replied, her eyes bright with humour. She tilted her head. "You know, purple looks good on you.

It suits your complexion."

"Well gee, thanks," he replied dryly, then gestured toward the snack table. "Want to grab a coffee? I think I see some shortbread cookies too. Somebody's started their Christmas baking already."

Anna pulled out her phone and her face fell. "I really should get going." She hesitated. "I'd love to stay longer, but I have a ton of work to do on that manuscript for Clarissa. She wants to send some proposals to publishers soon."

Right, her manuscript. He tried to push down the disappointment welling inside him. "Is this for *The Wicked Moon*, or your new story?"

"Oh, the new one isn't anywhere near ready yet." She sighed and pushed her glasses up her nose, then shoved her phone in her pocket. "I'm not sure what to do with it. I wrote a few more chapters, but it needs tweaking. I haven't even asked Clarissa if she's interested in it yet."

"Well, my offer is still there," Matthew replied. "If you want me to help with those first few chapters, we can shine them up so your agent will have no choice but to take it on."

She bit her lip, as if mulling over his proposition.

"Think about it and let me know. No pressure." He jerked his head toward the chairs, where their jackets and her purse sat. "Should we head out?"

"You can stay if you like. Don't leave just because I am."

Heated words from the snack table grabbed his attention. Joanne thrust her coffee-laden hand in Laura's direction, scowling, while Laura stamped her foot in response. Sue and the lady who'd been sitting beside her looked back and forth between them, thoroughly engrossed in the argument.

"Nah, I think I'll head out," he replied.

She followed his gaze and giggled. "Yeah, you wouldn't want to get caught in Joanne's crosshairs over the horror suggestion."

"Everybody has their favourite genres," he replied. "Though it's good to be open to new things too. You never know what might resonate with you."

"Touché." She tilted her head, then led the way to where they'd been sitting. They put on their jackets and with a wave to Christine and Laura, they made their way to the exit.

Matthew opened the door to the tinkling chimes and held it open for Anna. When she stepped into the crisp evening air, her sleek hair caught in the lamplight, and her breath created puffs of mist.

Suddenly self-conscious now that they were alone, Matthew rocked back on his heels. "I forgot to mention, your hair looks nice tonight. I mean, I like it messy too—"

"Messy?" Anna's cheeks turned pink.

Dude, why are you talking about her hair? He scratched the back of his neck and tried again. "I mean, I had fun tonight. I'm glad I joined a club for book nerds with you."

She burst out laughing and gently touched his forearm. "Right. I'm glad too." She tucked her scarf beneath the collar of her jacket, then her tone softened. "Umm, about your offer—"

"If you want me to stop bugging you about it, I will."

"No, it's not that." She glanced over her shoulder at the door, then stepped closer to him. A slight floral smell came over him. *What is that? Her shampoo?* It definitely smelled better than lavender. She looked up at him with those wide brown eyes, and he took a step back, fighting the urge to put his arm around her.

Whoa. Steady yourself, man.

She continued, "It's just, I was embarrassed. You saw my other book, and you didn't like it. What's to say you would like this one?"

That's what this is all about? I should have known. Of course, she didn't want him to see her new manuscript. He'd flat out rejected her work. No, even worse, he'd pulled the rug out from under what should have been her debut novel. He'd made every author's nightmare come true for her. Why would she trust him?

He cleared his throat and put his hands in his pockets. "I only want to help. I didn't suggest Ahmed reject your book because it wasn't any good. It was for the same reason your agent told you—books about fairies aren't selling well in adult fantasy right now. These trends, they come and go."

"I know," she replied, lowering her gaze. "And I'm sorry I was hard on you for it."

"I'm sorry I had a part in cancelling your book. If I'd have known—"

She shook her head. "That's the point. You shouldn't have known. It's your job, you can't play favourites based on an author's feelings." She paused, as if to brace herself. "I'd like to send you my chapters."

He raised his brows. *Just like that? She's going to trust me?* "What changed your mind?"

"Well, now that I got to know you a bit, you don't seem like the pompous business man my sister and I had you pegged for."

"Pompous?" *Okay, maybe I deserve that after what I said to Tad about my role with Raven Stone.* "Wait, you talked to your sister about me?"

"Of course, it's not every day you meet the man who ruined your dreams," she teased. She tucked her hair behind her ear and gave him an amused look, making him want to pull her into his arms right then and there. She straightened her tote bag around her shoulder. "Anyways, thanks for the nice evening. I should get going and let Monty out, then lock myself in with my computer until my shift tomorrow afternoon at the inn."

Matthew swept his gaze across the street to the Blooming Box and the dark window of her apartment. "How about I walk you to your door?"

"It's like, right there." She pointed to the dimly lit door next to the flower shop window. But then, she softened and slipped her arm through the crook of his elbow. "Although, I guess it is nice to be escorted across the street."

His arm tingled at her touch. He looked both ways and started across the street. "Like the little old lady you aspire to be, right?"

She giggled and pressed closer to him as they strode across the pavement. "I was thinking more of a queen, but I guess a little old lady is more accurate."

"Hmm, I think a queen sounds about right too."

They stopped in front of her door. Anna turned to face him, her arm still entwined with his, and a tress of her hair caught on the joint of her glasses. Without thinking, he gently brushed the hair aside. She looked up at him for a moment, and he was afraid he'd crossed a line. But instead of recoiling, she stepped closer, then stood on her toes and pressed her lips to his.

CHAPTER TWELVE

Anna stared through the raindrops on her windshield at the mass of merlot-coloured leaves that edged the front porch of the inn, only half listening to her sister's voice. Her phone sat on the dash on speaker mode, and Monty whined from his seat next to her. He leaned over to lick her face, leaving a streak of saliva on the lens of her glasses.

"Ugh, buddy." She rubbed his ears, then had him sit on his haunches.

"Anna?" Kelsey asked. "You okay?"

"I'm fine. Monty just tried to clean my glasses for me." Anna took them off and grabbed the microfibre cloth from her console to wipe them off.

"How are you holding up?"

"Well, it's seven-thirty on a Monday morning, I got barely any writing done this weekend, and I'm having a panic attack about going to work. So, not great." She put her glasses back on and closed her eyes. *Why did I have to kiss him? What was I thinking?*

"Take a deep breath," Kelsey replied. "It's okay. I mean, he kissed you back, right?"

"Definitely." Anna picked up her travel mug from the cupholder, wrapping her cold fingers around it for warmth, and thought back to Friday night—Matthew swooping in to help her save face with Jace and Jillian, then laughing and joking with him at the meeting. Even when he'd convinced her to stand up and receive her Page Turners pin from Christine, it had been exactly what she needed. For once, she'd relaxed and pushed the stress of fixing her book from her mind.

Then later, in the light of the streetlamp, with her arm tucked through his, and her body pressed against him when he touched her hair—it had all seemed so natural. *And that kiss*. Her cheeks warmed at the memory. She didn't know what had come over her, but he hadn't seemed to mind. She'd never been kissed like that before, as if he couldn't get enough of her.

For a moment, she'd felt like the heroine in her own novel.

But then they broke apart, and reality hit. This was Matthew—Madison's brother, her temporary co-worker, the man who had tore apart her work with no regard.

"I barely even said goodbye. I ran up the stairs and left him there on the sidewalk, looking completely confused."

"Oh, Anna."

"I'm a grown woman! What's wrong with me?"

"Did he reach out to you later?"

Anna opened the lid of her travel mug, breathing in the grassy scent of green tea. "Yes. Well, he sent me a text yesterday asking me how I was doing. I replied with *totally fine!* and three happy face emojis."

"Okay," Kelsey replied in an amused tone. "Then what?"

"He told me he had fun at the book club meeting. Then he gave me his email address to send my chapters to him."

"See, that's a good sign. You must not have scared him off. At least, not too badly."

"Kelsey."

She chuckled. "Oh, come on, Anna. It's not a big deal. You kissed. So what?"

"I have to work with him. And now, he's critiquing my work." Anna took a trembling sip of her tea. "It's going to be even worse if he doesn't like it. What if he lies to me about it? To avoid hurting my feelings or to try and get more action with me."

Kelsey snorted a laugh. "Is that what you call action? A peck on the street?"

"Not helpful, Kels."

"Right, I'm sorry." She paused. "Honestly, I think you're overthinking this. Just talk to him and see how he feels about what happened."

"How am I supposed to bring it up?" Anna raised her voice to a falsely cheerful tone. "*Hey, Matthew, so remember how I kissed you the other night?*"

"If you don't clear the air, it's going to be awkward working beside him for the next two weeks."

They were quiet for a moment, then Anna put down her tea and reached over and scratched Monty's ears. He bumped her hand with his nose in appreciation. "Okay. You're right. We're both adults here. I can figure this out."

"There you go. You got this."

The sound of crunching gravel met her ears. She looked in her rear-view mirror and saw Rodger's truck rumbling up the driveway.

"I better go, Kels. I still have to kennel Monty."

"Okay. Have a good day, and remember to relax."

Easier said than done. "Thanks. You have a good day too."

"Listening to cranky customers yell at me over the phone is never a good day," Kelsey replied dryly. "But it's a pay cheque, I guess. Thanks. Talk to you tonight for pizza supper."

Anna said goodbye, then hung up and clipped Monty's leash to his collar. She lifted the hood of her rain jacket, then let him out of the car and started toward the stable. As her boots squished over the soggy ground, she took a calming breath of the cool autumn air.

It'll be okay. I'll apologize and let him know I got caught up the moment. Smooth things over, so he can work on my story without it being weird. Her throat tightened at the thought of her word document sitting in his inbox. *Maybe he hasn't even looked at it yet.*

"This is disgusting." Anna pulled her rubber-gloved hand from the corner of the counter in the makeshift office of the barn, gripping the wire brush tightly. There were bird droppings everywhere and even with a mask on, she cringed at the thought of what kind particles must be flying around.

"Right?" Violet said from across the room, where she was sweeping feathers and droppings from the floor. She leaned on the broom handle, eyeing the mess around them. "I don't know how they think this is going to be a coat room in less than two weeks."

After cleaning the open area of the barn last week, Anna had felt confident in their mission to have it ready for the Starlight Dance. They'd managed to clear most of the muck, dust, and old hay from the main area. After a good pressure washing, even the messes from the birds and mice had been washed away. Anna had been able to envision the soft white lights, the tables with mahogany covers that Madison had told her about, and the bar area that Rodger and Matthew were putting together right now.

But that was before Rodger had led her and Violet to the office in the back corner. The room had been added years after the original owners built the barn, and it had no ceiling apart from the rafters above. Apparently, a whole flock of pigeons had taken to roosting there. While Rodger had pest control help him chase the birds off this summer, and the new tin roof helped keep them away, their old debris still coated the room. Anna wasn't sure if they should be cleaning it, or condemning it as a biohazard.

Violet set the broom against the wall and tugged off her gloves. "I need a break. Rodger has cold drinks in the truck, want to come get one with me?"

"Thanks, but I'll keep going for a bit. I have to leave in an hour to get ready for my shift in the kitchen. But you go ahead." Anna jammed the wire brush in the corner and swiped a pile of litter onto the floor.

"I'll bring some water back for you."

"Thanks, Violet."

Violet pulled open the door, causing the hinges to creak. "Oh hey, Matthew. I'm going to grab a water, do you want one?"

Anna stiffened. She hadn't had a chance to talk to Matthew yet this morning, not properly anyways. After putting Monty away, she'd rushed over to the barn. Matthew had already started measuring a spot for the rustic wood bar area he and Rodger were building that day, and she'd immediately joined Violet in the back room.

Matthew moved aside to let Violet pass, then stepped into the room. "Sure, thanks. I added some Cokes to the cooler in his back seat. If you want one, help yourself."

"Really? Thanks!"

Violet's footsteps faded away.

Matthew rested his gaze on Anna and ran a hand through his disheveled hair. A thin layer of sawdust coated his flannel shirt and jeans. "Hey, thought I'd grab a moment to talk with you before you left today."

Anna adjusted her glasses, which were filled with fog from wearing her mask. *It's not fair. He still looks amazing after a morning of work, and I'm here with mask lines on my face, covered in debris, like some sort of alien disaster.* "Sure. Let's go outside. It's disgusting in here."

He held the door open. "After you, fellow Page Turner."

Her tension eased at his teasing grin, then she stepped out of the room and tore the mask from her face. She shoved it in her sweater pocket and glanced at the open barn area, where Violet and Rodger were chatting with drinks in their hands. "Let's go out the back."

He nodded and followed her through the back door and into the field behind the barn. Two horses stood beneath the bright red leaves of a nearby maple tree, gently swishing their tails with their eyes half-closed. The rain had let up, and the sky had cleared to finally reveal the sun.

Anna's gaze fell on the horses, and her lips curled into a smile.

Matthew closed the door behind them, then stepped through the brown grass to stand with her. "You like horses?"

"Yes. Well, sort of. My mom used to make my sister and I take riding lessons. My sister was a natural, but I hated it. I was always afraid I couldn't control my horse. The only part I liked was in the winter, when the stable we rode at would have sleigh rides."

"Sounds magical."

"It was, actually. One of my favourite childhood memories." She sighed dreamily. "That's one thing I miss about Alberta. The snow. I'm sure they've had loads of it by now."

"That sounds *cold*."

She giggled, and he was quiet for a moment. Then he cleared his throat, giving her a sideways glance. "So, about the other night."

Anna pushed her hair from her forehead and tried to lay it flat, wishing they'd had this conversation earlier, before she was covered in sweat and grime. "Oh, yeah. I'm sorry. I didn't mean to make things awkward."

"You don't have anything to be sorry for, Anna."

"I don't want it to be weird between us."

He scratched his chin, giving her a roguish smile that made her want to kiss him again. "Weird seems to be our thing, right from day one."

"You're not wrong about that."

He chuckled and put his hands in his pockets, rocking back on his heels. "Look, I just got out of a serious relationship a few months ago. I wasn't expecting to meet somebody new so quickly."

Oh, this is how it's going to be. The old, "I'm not ready for a relationship" thing. Anna lifted her chin, avoiding his gaze. "I get it. Honestly, it was only a stupid impulse. It won't happen again."

"No, that's not—"

"You don't want to start anything. And that's fine. Jace and I broke up pretty recently too. This summer. So I probably shouldn't—"

Matthew held up his hands. "Whoa. Hang on. That's not what I'm getting at."

Anna took a breath, trying to ground herself. Despite the sun casting a golden glow over the pasture, a cold breeze swept over them and she hugged her elbows. "Sorry. Go on."

"I wanted to see how you're feeling about things," he said. "I know we got off on the wrong foot. The whole thing about *I'm a big mean editor and you're the author whose dreams I crushed*. But I had a lot of fun with you on Friday. More than I've had with somebody in a long time."

Anna took in the serious look on his face. For once, his eyes weren't crinkled with laughter. The joke she'd expected he was about to make didn't come.

She blinked. "I did too."

"I was thinking, maybe we should go out sometime. On a real date."

She tilted her head. "You mean hanging out in a bookshop arguing over what to read with the book club ladies, sitting near my ex and his girlfriend, wasn't a real date?"

"I guess you can call it that. But maybe the next one should be a little more conventional. Maybe something like dinner at a nice restaurant this weekend?"

She hesitated for a moment, wondering if this was a good idea. *What if things don't work out between us? He's Madison's brother, he has the start of my new story in his hands. I should be spending my time writing, not running around with a guy—*

"Anna?"

She met his gaze, and her resistance melted away. "Sure. I have Friday evening off, as usual. I don't know the Fraser Valley that well yet, so if you have somewhere in mind, I'm in."

"Great, I'll pick you up around six. There are a few places in Abbotsford we could check out—"

The barn door scraped open behind them, and

Anna turned to see Violet pop her head outside. "Hey, sorry to interrupt. But, uh, the dogs are out again."

"What?" Anna put a hand on her hip. "I'm sure I tied that rope around the gate post. How did they get out?"

"I don't know, but Uncle Rodger said to get you to round them up." She gestured to Matthew. "And he also said to tell you that he needs help unloading the new bar from the truck."

Matthew gave her a wave. "I'm on it. Thanks for letting us know, Violet." He looked at Anna. "Need help rounding up the dogs first?"

Anna wrinkled her nose. "Nah, go help Rodger. I can handle the runaway mutts."

"If you're sure—"

"I am." She motioned toward the door, then followed him inside with her gaze lingering on his broad shoulders.

A real date. With Matthew. I hope this is a good idea. Her chest tingled and for once, she didn't push that hope away.

Chapter Thirteen

Matthew stared at the laptop before him, shifting his seat in the hard oak chair at Marshal's kitchen table. Anna's manuscript filled the screen. The first line was a zinger. He was instantly hooked by the main character's turmoil as she watched her sister teeter on the brink of death on a narrow mountain ridge, her heavy backpack and gravity threatening to win the conflict at any second.

This is pretty good. Why wouldn't her agent want it? A sale is a sale, even if it's not her niche genre. He'd been looking at Anna's chapters for almost an hour, typing notes into the margins, trying to be honest but more sensitive than he'd been with other clients before. *If she made it clearer from the beginning why the main characters haven't spoken for two years, really dig us into the first sister's feelings, I think the hook would work.*

He'd been taught by the senior editor at Raven Stone to edit ruthlessly, that it would teach the authors work ethic and to grow a thick skin. But maybe there was a better way to do things. To critique in a constructive manner, while encouraging the author to build upon their strengths. He remembered what Brittany had said to him when she broke things off, that he could be thoughtless and inconsiderate. That she needed somebody more *sensitive.*

He closed Anna's document, a knot in his stomach. Maybe Brittany had been right. He hadn't exactly been a doting boyfriend, often poring over manuscripts rather than going to after-work social hour with Brittany and her friends. He'd even missed her mother's birthday dinner, which he hadn't felt was that big of a deal at the time. *But it had been to her. That's the point.*

Still, that's no excuse to dump me over a text message. She couldn't even do it in person, and now she expects me to read her emails?

He tapped his fingers on the handle of his empty coffee mug, eyeing the glass vase filled with some sort of orange flowers that sat in the centre of the table. His mouth twitched at the gesture from Sophie. Along with tea in the cupboard, a tidy pantry, and a proper mail organizer, her touch was everywhere around here. And he had to admit, he liked her effect on Marshal. Even while struggling with getting this greenhouse built, a phone call from her would always melt his scowl into a smile. It had never been like that between Matthew and Brittany.

His mind wandered to Anna, and the way she poked fun at him at the book club meeting as if they were old friends. He'd known her for only a week, yet somehow it felt like much longer. The second he'd seen her coming out of that inn, walking toward him in the rain, a spark of attraction had lit inside him. And then, he'd gone and ruined it with his big mouth, bragging to Tad about his job. *Did I have to sound like such a jerk?*

But things seemed better between them now. More than better, actually. Friday night, when Anna kissed him, that spark had flared into a flame.

Something inside him had aligned, but before he could kiss her again, she'd said goodbye and was already making her way up to her apartment.

Despite the cool demeanor he tried to maintain, he'd been beside himself all weekend while helping Marshal finish setting up the garden boxes in his greenhouse. At his parents' weekly family dinner on Sunday evening, the thought of Anna sitting next to him at the table didn't make him freak out, which was weird... and interesting. But before he invited her to a family dinner, they had to have some solo meals first—after all, all they did was share an impulsive kiss. Hardly a reason to ask her to meet his parents. Even if she did know them a bit already.

He clicked out of his client files and opened his web browser, then typed in a search for restaurants in the area. Cedar Lake didn't have a lot of options—Josie's Diner, a few fast-food restaurants, the Last Call pub... He didn't want to take Anna out for pub food though, and the inn was not an option. He was sure the last place she wanted to eat would be her workplace, with Sophie and Tad hovering around. *No. Absolutely not.*

As he skimmed through the list of restaurants in nearby towns, an email notification popped up in the corner of his screen. He clicked over to his inbox, and there beneath the survey for the Page Turners, the name Brittany Holt glared at him in bold letters. The subject line read, *One last chance.*

He frowned and scrubbed his jaw with his palm. *One last chance for what? For us? No, we're over. Isn't she with Frank now?* He couldn't imagine what she wanted. She'd made it clear she was done, and he was grateful for it now. *Whatever, may as well see what she has to say.* He opened the email.

Hey Matthew,

I don't know if you've been reading these, but I really hope this one gets through. I know this is weird, but again, I wanted to say I'm sorry with the way we left things back in Toronto. I'd been wanting to talk for a long time, and I let it go on for far too long. When I reached the end of my rope, a text was all I could do. I am sorry for that. I could have handled it better.

Like I said in my previous emails, I'm coming to Vancouver for a business trip next week, and I was wondering if I could pop out to that little hometown of yours for lunch. Obviously, I'd like to talk and give us some closure, but I have an interesting business proposition for you too. I can email you some information if you like. The job would be in Vancouver, so not far from your family.

Please let me know, so I can stop harassing you.

Britt

Matthew bit back a low growl. *Britt? As if we're buddies now? Fat chance.* He reread the email with guilt pricking his skin. Maybe they did owe each other some closure. As soon as she'd broken it off, he'd blocked her number and avoided any of her typical hangouts. He'd moved to Cedar Lake without even telling her, though somebody must have. He gritted his teeth. *Probably Frank.*

The new business opportunity was intriguing, however. He'd checked this morning and his profile with Editors Canada was live for potential clients to browse, and he had written a proof of a discount offer he could send to Anna to share with her author friends. While he'd gained motivation to get his freelance career rolling, a stable pay cheque was still alluring. Especially one in Vancouver, close to his parents. To Madison and Marshal.

And Anna. His throat tightened. *No, I can't think like that. I barely know her yet. I rushed into things with Brittany, and look where that got me. I need to take things slow with her.*

He typed Brittany a curt email, asking for more information about the job, then tabbed over to his professional website. He frowned at the boring white screen with his name and credentials. *No wonder I'm not getting any work. I can't let Anna send this to potential clients. It's horrible, as if I don't even know how to run a computer.* And the truth was, he didn't. He had no idea to make his website look more appealing.

The front door banged shut, and Marshal's heavy footsteps thumped down the hallway. He entered the kitchen and flicked on the light. "A bit dark in here, isn't it?"

"I work better in the dark." Matthew twisted in his chair. Dirt streaked his brother's face, and his clothes were caked with mud. "You just get out of a mud wrestling competition?"

"Dylan dumped a load of dirt outside the greenhouse door. He told me he knew how to run a bobcat, but I should have known better. We had to hand shovel it into the boxes." The look he gave Matthew warned him not to ask further questions. "I'll go strip down at the washing machine downstairs. Want to have a beer and play *Fallout* after I shower? I could use a few hours of shooting ghouls."

"You bet," Matthew replied. "I'm almost done here."

Marshal peered over Matthew's shoulder at the screen and frowned. "You know, Dylan might be able to help you with that." Matthew wasn't exactly sure what Madison's boyfriend did for a living, but it was in the realm of computer sciences and information technology.

"It's not very good, is it?"

"Not really," Marshal agreed. "You should take a look at the farm's page, Morning Harvest dot com. Dylan had a photographer come out and everything, and he even designed an online order form I can check from my phone."

Matthew pulled it up, and a photo of Marshal holding a basket of carrots popped up on the screen. "Well, look at you. A real Mr. McGregor. Chase any rabbits lately?"

"Excuse me?"

"Peter Rabbit? Beatrix Potter?"

Marshal shook his head. "I have no idea what you're talking about."

"Mom read the books to us when we were kids."

Marshal waved him off and walked toward the hallway, leaving a trail of dirt behind him. He paused at the entrance. "Hey, what are you doing this weekend?"

"I'm having dinner with someone on Friday, why?"

"Who?"

"Does it matter?"

Marshal raised his brows. "I guess not. Just curious." He leaned his shoulder against the door frame. "Sophie and I are heading out for the weekend. I was wondering if you'd mind watching the place."

"She convinced you to go away?" Matthew feigned a shocked expression. "What can't that woman do? Where are you going?"

"We're heading to a cabin in the Okanagan valley for a couple nights. She was able to call a friend who's a chef to fill in for her."

"That's great, Marsh. I never thought I'd see the day you'd step foot off this farm for more than a few hours. It's good, you deserve the break."

Matthew stood from his chair and stretched his back. "I can take care of things here. There isn't that much to do over the weekend, is there?"

"Well," Marshal scratched his ear, "there's going to be chickens to look after."

"What? Like, live chickens?"

Marshal nodded. "Sophie's been talking about laying hens for weeks. She'd love farm-fresh eggs for the inn, and for some reason she actually likes the flappy things. They're going to be her pet project."

"She doesn't even live here."

Marshal shrugged. "It doesn't matter. I can scatter some chicken feed around in the mornings. Can't be that hard. Beena and I cleaned out Grandpa's old coop today. All the supplies were in there, and the structure is still in good shape. I bedded it down with straw from the garden, and I have some laying hens being delivered on Thursday."

Matthew bit back a laugh at the thought of Marshal looking after chickens. He'd always been afraid of birds, ever since their mom's old pet parakeet had escaped its cage and dive bombed his head when they were kids. "Alright, I can throw some feed for them."

"Thanks." Marshal straightened. "Don't tell Sophie. It's a surprise. I'll show her on Sunday when we get back."

"My lips are sealed, Mr. Tweedy."

"What is with the names tonight?"

Matthew laughed and bent over to shut down his computer. "Come on, you haven't seen *Chicken Run*?"

Marshal furrowed his brows. "Right. But for the record, Sophie's a lot nicer than that Mrs. Tweedy. A lot better looking too."

"Ha!" Matthew grinned and made his way to the fridge to grab a beer. "That's true, I'll give you that."

"See you in a few minutes. Be prepared to actually protect the compound this time, okay? Instead of daydreaming about whoever you're taking to dinner." Marshal headed downstairs to the laundry area, and Matthew wandered to the living room.

He's one to talk. Matthew plopped down on the saggy green couch across from the big screen TV. He cracked his beer. It hissed, and he took a sip, enjoying the savoury taste. *Flowers on the table. Going on vacations. Raising chickens.*

He shook his head, then caught himself thinking of Anna and his desire to spend an evening at home with her.

Was he actually jealous of Marshal's relationship with Sophie? His stomach knotted. *It's pretty nice, I guess. With the right woman.* Was Anna the right woman for him? She was definitely a better fit than Brittany. But despite Brittany's faults, he'd been the one to drive her away without even being aware of it. Could he trust himself to do better with Anna? To give her what she deserved?

Ease off the gas, buddy, or you'll ruin things before they even begin.

Chapter Fourteen

Anna ran the paint roller over the wood slats of the barn wall before her, covering up the faded brown with a darker streak of stain. A rock song played from the radio on the now-clean counter of the back room. The destroyed linoleum on the floor had been pulled up to reveal the concrete beneath, which Anna and Violet would paint in a few days. There was no sign or smell of pigeons or mice or debris. They had worked hard the last few days, and it was beginning to believably look like a coat room.

Matthew drilled one last screw into place on the wall-length metal hanging rod he'd just installed, then took a step back to admire his work. "You know, for a guy with a desk job, I don't think I did too bad." He gave the coat rack a satisfied pat with his free hand.

"Violet will be impressed when she comes in tomorrow." Anna dipped her roller in the paint tray at her feet. "Hopefully her driving exam went well this morning."

"She told me yesterday to watch for her driving her mom's Escalade," Matthew said.

"I think her hopes are much too high," Anna said with a laugh. "If her mom's anything like Katie, she'll be lucky to drive a beat-up old work truck."

Matthew chuckled and rolled up the sleeves of his hooded sweatshirt. "I'm going to pack up these tools, and then I'll be out of your hair."

Anna ran the paint roller up the wall in front of her, careful to make sure she caught the edges of the rough-cut lumber. "No rush. You're not in my way." She gave him a sideways glance. "Besides, I kind of like the company."

"Only kind of?" Matthew began to wrap up the cord from the power drill.

"I mean, you're no Violet, but—"

"Ha, ha." He placed the drill in the old milk crate he'd used to haul the tools, then pulled his phone from his pocket and frowned at the screen.

"Something wrong?" Anna asked.

He shrugged and slid the cell into his pocket. "It's my mom. I'll call her back when we take a break later. I'm sure she's got some job postings to tell me about."

Anna stopped painting and turned to face him, holding the roller in front of her. "Again? Well, you're not alone."

"What do you mean?"

She raised a brow. "Meddling mothers. Mine is determined to make me return to Calgary and have me work for her corporation."

"Wow, a real bigwig huh?"

"Yup. She's the Vice President of King Oilfield Construction. Been there since she was like twenty-five, a single mother with a toddler and a baby to care for, climbing the corporate ladder."

"That's actually pretty impressive."

Anna sighed and placed her roller on the edge of the paint tray. "Sure is. But she's not too pleased with her daughters not living up to her legacy." She waved a hand. "Anyways, it's not a big deal. I've met your mom. I don't think she's as condescending as mine."

Matthew cocked his head. "Maybe not. But she has her expectations for us kids too, and I've never lived up to them. Her dream was for me to be a doctor like my dad, but science was never my strong point."

"Let me guess, you were more into English too?"

"Of course. Writing and literature always came naturally to me." He sat on the edge of the milk crate and put his elbows on his knees. "I never tried very hard in school though. I was having too much fun running around with my friends." He cocked a brow. "I bet you were always a real book nerd."

She adjusted her glasses and gave him a proud look. "Of course. I was always that quiet kid. And to this day, I'd rather explore an old bookstore or sit in a café with my laptop than go to parties or big events."

"You know, I'm the same way now," he said with a laugh. "My ex, Brittany, was all about going out to clubs and staying out late. It was one of our biggest issues."

Anna shifted her weight, unsure of what to say. "Well, sometimes things just don't work out."

"You got that right," he agreed. "Hey, speaking of being a book nerd—how are things going with your fantasy manuscript?"

She sighed, then pulled over the step ladder she'd been using to reach the high portions of the walls and sat on the top rung. "I'm still trying to age it down to YA. It's not going well, though. I've never written for teens before. I got some advice from a friend who has, but it still doesn't feel quite right."

"Do you want to write for teens?"

"Not really."

"So, then why are you even trying?"

"Well," she said slowly, "my agent knows the industry better than I do. If I want to be published and build an author career, I should listen to her advice. Don't you think?"

Matthew shrugged. "From what you've said, your agent knows her stuff. But the thing is, you might pigeonhole yourself as a YA writer. You don't want to get stuck there if that's not what you want to write."

Anna sucked in a breath. *I hadn't thought of that. I don't want to get stuck writing stories I'm not passionate about.* She thought back to the agonizing months she spent waiting for responses from agents, only to be let down time and time again.

After Clarissa had agreed to work with her, she'd thought she had finally made it. And when things fell apart, she'd hung on tightly, trying to force it to work.

But what if that's what it takes to get published? Where's the line between learning and improving your craft and losing your authenticity as a writer? She glanced at Matthew. "That gives me a lot to think about, thank you. It's so hard to get an agent, it took years and dozens of queries. I'm afraid to lose her."

He clasped his hands together. "You did it once, so you know you can do it again. Besides, once you send her your new project, she might bite. I looked at your chapters last night, and you've got a great story brewing there. I think you could do something with it."

She bit the side of her cheek, taking in his words. *Maybe he's right. Maybe I should put away* The Wicked Moon *for now and focus on my mountain story*. A swell of panic pushed against her at the thought. All those years, all that hard work perfecting her book, convincing an agent to take a chance on it—could it all have been for nothing?

What would my mom think? Her stomach tightened. *Would I have to move home and take a full-time job again, with Mom hovering over my shoulder, trying to push me into a 'real' career while trying to write?* She didn't think she could do it.

"Those are my thoughts," Matthew straightened in his seat and shrugged. "It's up to you to decide though." He paused. "You know, I have an agent friend who is interested in women's fiction stories like yours. I'll email you my notes tonight. If you edit those chapters and shine them up, I could send them her way to see what she thinks."

Anna's throat thickened. She wasn't sure it was ready. She'd barely started the manuscript. It wasn't even fully plotted. Yet, she already knew where it was going. Internally, she was sure of the points she wanted to hit and how the story would end. It had come a lot more naturally for her than *The Wicked Moon*—which scared her, in a way. Could something that flowed so easily in the beginning really be any good?

She swallowed. "Maybe. I'll go through your notes tonight and get back to you."

He gave her an understanding nod and got to his feet. "You bet. Just let me know." He bent to check over the tools, then looked over his shoulder at her. "Oh yeah, about Friday—Marshal and Sophie are taking off on a little getaway, so I'll have the house to myself. I was wondering if, instead of a stuffy restaurant, you'd like a home-cooked dinner?"

Anna tucked her hair behind her ear, pushing the thoughts of her writing away. She'd been thinking about their date since he'd asked her, aching for the work week to end. She'd already picked out the perfect dress, her teal-blue one that showed off her small waist and shoulders. And maybe that necklace her mother gave her a few years ago—the one with the teardrop pendant.

Now, her chest fluttered at the idea of an intimate dinner with him. Alone at his house, without the hustle and bustle of a busy restaurant. A better chance to get to know him more, and maybe this time a real kiss that didn't involve her freaking out afterwards. "That sounds amazing. That is, as long as I'm not the one doing the cooking. Fridays are my break from kitchen work."

"That would be pretty rude of me to invite you over and ask you to cook."

"Can you?"

"Can I what?"

"Cook?" she teased.

"Of course. I can grill a pretty mean steak." He gave her a wry grin that made her want to step into his arms right there in the coat room.

The sound of a phone vibrating hummed through the air, and Matthew jerked his gaze from hers and pulled out his cell again. He frowned at the screen. "I should probably take this one."

"No problem." She stood from her perch on the stepladder and stretched her arms. "I should probably finish up this wall and get ready to go, anyways."

He tipped his head to her. As he strode toward the door, he held his phone to his ear. "Hey, Brittany."

He stepped out of the room and closed the door behind him.

Brittany? A knot formed in Anna's stomach. *Isn't that his ex-girlfriend? He still talks to her?* She grabbed her paint roller and dipped it the stain at the end of the tray. *It's not a big deal. I'm sure there's an explanation.*

But her mind wandered to thoughts of Jace, of how he assured her there was nothing between him and Jillian anymore. *And then he dumped me to go back to her.*

She dropped the paint roller's handle and took out her phone, searching for a distraction. An email notification blinked on her screen, and she tapped it open to see a message from her mother.

Hi Anna,

Please see the attached information about the data entry job and the confirmation of your tele-interview next Wednesday. I submitted your resumé to our human resources department, and they are interested in talking to you. You'll need to find three references. Hopefully your current boss at that casual inn job will be willing to vouch for you.

Let me know you received this. If you'd like some coaching for the interview, I can try to set aside time this weekend to have a virtual call.

Anna gripped the phone with trembling fingers, staring at the screen in disbelief. *She submitted my resumé? Without even talking to me?* She turned off the phone and jammed it in her pocket, fuming. *Is that even legal?*

She grabbed the paint roller and slapped it on the wall, causing the stain to splatter the front of her hoodie. But she didn't care. Her mom had crossed the line this time. And she would—well, she would send her a firmly worded email stating she was not moving back to Calgary any time soon.

She paused mid-paint stroke, fear washing over her. *Or should I just do the interview? My writing situation is a mess with no guarantees or a clear way out. And after this barn is done, I'll be looking for work again.* She swallowed, tears stinging her eyes.

As much as she hated to admit it, maybe her mom was right. *Time to get your head out of the clouds and grow up, Anna.* Her heart pricked at the mere idea of moving away from Cedar Lake. Leaving the quiet countryside, her new friends, and the inn that had come to feel like home. And what about Matthew? Things were just starting to go their way.

She'd never thought doing the responsible thing would feel so wrong.

Chapter Fifteen

Matthew set down his coffee mug on the kitchen table, engrossed in the revised opening scene of Anna's manuscript. The main character, Eve, stood frozen on the edge, terrified to continue. Her sister moved across in front of her with purposeful strides, not showing even a glimmer of fear. Anna's prose and details were even more gripping than before, and her words flowed seamlessly from the page.

This is really good. She took my suggestions and made them even better. He finished the scene, then clicked over to the email Anna had sent him.

Hi Matthew,

I think I'd like to take you up on your offer to send these chapters to your agent friend. Do you think they're ready for her appraisal? I'm not sure about the flashback to the sisters' falling out. Let me know.

Also, I know your website isn't ready, but I passed your email along to my friend Scott. His sci-fi novel was cut from Raven Stone too, and he's thinking about self-publishing it and would like to speak to an editor soon. I hope that's okay.

Thanks again for helping me with this.

Anna

He typed her a quick reply, letting her know that he was thrilled she passed along his contact information, and that he loved the fixes she'd made and was sure they were ready to send to Dana. Then he found the original response he'd received from the agent, telling him she'd love to take a look at Anna's chapters. He wrote her a response, attached Anna's manuscript along with his own observations about the text, then hit send.

There. If anything, she'll respond with more notes on how to improve it. But he was sure Anna's work would pique her interest. Two sisters and their tribulations, healing the wounds of their childhood on a quest through nature, and working together to overcome the odds—this was the kind of story Dana would eat up.

And maybe, I'll finally have a client lined up soon. His mood lifted at the thought. *Some real work. Something I'm passionate about.*

His stomach rumbled, and he got up from the table to search for leftovers in the fridge. He swung open the door and eyed the contents—a day-old ham-and-cheese sandwich, a half-empty bottle of ketchup, a container of milk, and a box of beer. *For a produce farmer, the lack of vegetables in this house is alarming.*

There was no way he could make anything with these. It was as much his fault as his brother's, though. Between working at the inn, helping with the greenhouse, and editing Anna's story, he hadn't made the time to run to town for groceries. And Marshal was swamped too. It was no wonder they were living off take-out and pizza lately, like true bachelors.

I'll see what Marshal has on hand in the shop for produce, then pick up some nice steaks from the butcher shop. He'd already saved some online recipes for a kale salad and oven-roasted herbed potatoes. *Maybe dessert would be nice too. I can stop by Josie's Diner to pick up some of her famous cheesecake.*

He grabbed the sandwich and shut the fridge door, and the sound of a car rolling up the driveway caught his attention. Marshal had left only an hour ago to get supplies for his and Sophie's trip. He wouldn't be home this quickly. Matthew set his paltry meal on the counter and went to the window above the sink to see who it was. His mom's white SUV rolled up to the house, and the driver's door opened. A set of crutches swung from the vehicle to the ground.

What's Mom doing here? Matthew strode down the hall to the front porch and pulled on his boots. He stepped outside, letting the door slam shut behind him. By the time he got there, Paula was thumping her crutches on the steps, struggling to maneuver herself with a plastic container tucked under one arm.

"Mom, what are you doing? Let me help you."

She frowned with determination. "I can do it. Give me a second—"

"I'll take the container. Geez, Mom." He reached out, and she begrudgingly handed him the Tupperware. "What is this?"

"Homemade potato salad and two pork chops.

Madison went for dinner with Dylan, and I made too much for your dad and me. I thought you and Marshal would appreciate the leftovers."

His lips twitched with a grin. *Right, she happened to make two extra pork chops, knowing full well that it was only her and dad tonight?* Nevertheless, he appreciated the gesture, and so did his growling stomach.

"Thanks, Mom. Marshal's not home, but I'm sure I can finish his half too."

She gave him a dry look, then leaned on her crutches and tried to hop up the first stair on her good foot.

"Wait. You're going to sprain your other ankle." He took her elbow with his free hand and helped her hobble up the remaining steps and into the house.

He led the way down the hallway and into the kitchen, then pulled out a chair for her at the table. He closed his laptop and set it on the island in the middle of the room, then grabbed the sandwich from the counter and put it and the container of leftovers in the fridge.

"Want anything to drink?" He gestured at the half-filled coffee pot. "I have coffee on, or I could make you some tea."

"It's too late in the day for coffee." Paula leaned her crutches against the table, then twisted in her seat to rest her sprained ankle on the chair across from her. "And since when is Marshal a tea drinker?"

"Since he started dating Sophie," Matthew replied. He made his way to the cupboard above the coffeemaker and opened it. "There's English breakfast, green jasmine, or a herbal blend with chamomile."

"English breakfast with a bit of cream would be nice."

"Milk okay?" He grabbed the box of tea and set it on the counter, then pulled a mug from one of the hooks on the wall next to the oven and dropped a tea bag into it.

"Even better." She eyed the vase of orange flowers on the table, then pulled it closer to her and gave the blooms a sniff. "These are pretty. Sophie's doing, too, I assume?"

"You got it. Her feminine touch is all over this house." He filled the copper kettle from the tap and set it on the stove to boil, then sat across from her at the table.

His mom smiled and set the flowers aside. "She's sure been good for him, that Sophie. You know, you need to find a girl like her. Now that Madison has Dylan—"

"You already have prospects for upcoming weddings and grandbabies, if that's what you're after." Matthew gave her a teasing grin, trying to avoid the topic. He couldn't tell her about his date with Anna. Not yet. *She'd probably show up here and invite Anna to Sunday family dinner*. He wasn't ready for that, and he was pretty sure Anna wasn't either.

Paula pressed her lips together. "There's nothing wrong with wanting to see my kids happy."

"Of course," he replied. "And I am happy. I have a few things to figure out, but I'll get back on track."

"Like your career?"

"Yes, like my career. I'm on it, though. Don't worry so much."

She reached into her jeans pocket and pulled out a rumpled newspaper clipping, then slid it across the table to him. He picked it up and read, "Editor wanted for Cedar Lake Community Post." He set it down in front of her. "A newspaper job ad? What is this, 1995? Do they even have a print paper anymore?"

"Read it," Paula urged, thrusting it back to him. "They do, but they also have a website and social media that needs to be maintained."

The kettle began to whistle, and Matthew pushed his chair back and got to his feet. He went to the stove to move the kettle from the burner and turn off the heat. The last thing he wanted to do was edit local news stories and manage social media. His passion lay in fiction, not in the coverage of a small town's summer softball league.

Besides, there was the potential client Anna was sending his way. And after talking to Brittany a few days ago, he'd also been mulling over the potential of a line editing job with a new press in Vancouver. Sure, he'd have to move there. But it was only a couple hours drive from home, much better than heading back east where most of the big-name publishers were located.

He had options. Ones that didn't include working for a tiny newspaper.

He poured hot water over the tea bag in the mug, then grabbed a spoon and the jug of milk and brought it to the table for her. "Thanks, Mom. I appreciate you looking out for me, but I'm not a newspaper editor. It's not my thing."

"I don't understand the difference," Paula said with a

huff. She dumped some milk in her steaming mug, gave it a stir, then removed the tea bag and lay it in the head of the spoon on the table. "I thought this was perfect. A job right in Cedar Lake—you said you wanted to be around more, like Marshal."

Like Marshal. Of course, he's always been the reliable one. Matthew's chest tightened, and he took the seat across from her again. "I do, Mom. But I'm not Marshal. I don't have an attachment to this town the way he does. It's you, and Dad, and Madison that I'm attached to." He paused, catching her eye. "And Marshal too. He's okay, I guess."

"Honey—"

"I can't take a job I'm not interested in. And you know, newspapers and media have totally different editing rules than fiction. I know a little bit, but I'd need more training. My BA is in English, not journalism."

"Well, it sounds like there's no option for you to stay in Cedar Lake at all then."

He leaned his elbows on the table, trying to give her a reassuring look. "Maybe not. If freelancing from home was a sure thing, I would put all my eggs in that basket. But starting out in that world is tough, Mom.

I need to make a living." He hesitated, catching the worried look on her face. He thought about sharing the potential lead from Anna with her, but what if it fell through? He was sure she'd be overexcited with the prospect of his own business getting some traction. No, he'd wait until he'd signed an actual contract.

"I know you do, dear."

"If I take an in-house job, finding one in Vancouver is my priority. I promise, I won't move so far away this time." He swallowed, not sure if he should mention the opportunity with Brittany either. He hadn't decided yet. But his mom was clearly having a hard time with things, and he wanted to ease her mind. "I have an interesting in opportunity in Vancouver—"

His mom's face lit up, and she opened her mouth to speak, but he held up his hand.

"Hang on. I'm not sure I'm going to take it." He shifted uneasily, wondering how she'd react to the fact that Brittany was involved. "Brittany contacted me, and she's starting with a new publishing company in Vancouver next week. They're opening in January, and they need a line editor. She recommended me for the job."

His mom pursed her lips, then took a sip of her tea and set it on the table. "Why would Brittany want to work with you again?"

"She's confident in my work," he replied slowly. He'd had the exact same question when they spoke on the phone. "She said she felt bad for how things ended, and wants to make amends. As friends, or maybe coworkers."

"Do you think that's wise?"

"She doesn't want me back, Mom. And even if she did, there's no way I'd consider it." That, he was absolutely sure of. Even if things hadn't ended poorly, they weren't a good match. They would never be able to make each other happy, and his feelings for her had shifted the moment he'd received her break-up text. "But the job is a good opportunity. And it's a lot closer to home than Toronto or New York."

Paula let out a sigh, then took another drink of her tea. "Okay. You're right. Vancouver is better." She paused, tapping her fingers against the rim of her mug. "But I hope you keep trying to freelance. I know it's not easy, but you're passionate about your work. Maybe Dylan could help you, he's contracting now."

Matthew leaned back in his chair, thinking about his ancient-looking website. *I'm almost as bad as the Cedar Lake Post and their physical job postings.* "That is still an option," he said. "Marshal showed me his farm website and mentioned that Dylan would probably be willing to help me with mine."

"Well, why haven't you asked him yet?" Paula replied. "Get on it. And if there's anything your dad and I can do, let us know." She tapped her finger on the newspaper clipping on the table. "I'll try to be better. Just talk to me."

"You're right," he said. "I haven't exactly been forthcoming with you and Dad about what I'm planning to do, but I don't have a firm answer yet." He paused. "I'll shoot Dylan a text tonight."

His mom straightened in her chair, looking pleased. "See? I'm not completely useless when it comes to helping my kids, even though they're adults."

"Sure, Mom," he said with a chuckle, but his thoughts were still on his job situation. The job proposal from Brittany was tempting—a full-time salary, benefits, and some stability in his life. But freelancing as an editor had its perks too, and with a little help from Dylan and Anna, maybe it could work. And what that would mean—it was almost too good to be true. *Freedom. Staying in Cedar Lake with my family. Pursuing something more with Anna.*

What would happen with her if he moved to Vancouver? He hated the thought of cutting things off before they even began. Would she be willing to try dating long distance? He frowned. Was that even fair to ask of her when they'd only met a couple short weeks ago?

His mom began to tell him about her plans for the Starlight Dance—something about the milk canisters and the dozen spools of burlap she'd picked up from the fabric store. He wondered if Anna would be going. He'd assumed so, since she worked at the inn. But didn't she work Saturday nights in the kitchen? And if she wasn't working, she'd probably be staying home to work on that overhaul of her fantasy manuscript. But still, the thought of spending another evening with her, maybe even asking her to dance, was tempting.

I'll ask her tomorrow.

"Matthew? Are you listening?"

He straightened and focused his attention on his mom. "Yes, sorry. You were saying something about the food? Sophie's black forest cupcakes?"

"Yes, they're to die for." Paula clasped her hands together on the table. "You have to try them. They're Marshal's favourite."

Matthew pressed his lips together and shook his head. *The more things change…*

But she'd brought him pork chops. And he definitely intended to eat Marshal's share.

Chapter Sixteen

Anna leaned back in her chair and sighed, thoroughly satisfied from the meal Matthew had prepared. Between the perfectly cooked steak, herbed potatoes, and the kale and cranberry salad, he'd certainly proved his proficiency in the kitchen. The pink and orange flowers on the table and the tidy farmhouse only added to the pleasant atmosphere.

She gazed into the kitchen area, where Matthew stood loading the dishwasher with Monty sitting next to him. The dog looked longingly at the dirty dishes but kept a polite distance. She'd tried to help clear the table, but Matthew had insisted on cleaning everything up, stating that she could cook for him next time.

She dreamily thought of having him over at her apartment, sharing dinner and maybe a bottle of wine, hiding out together from the cold winter rain outside.

"So," she said, pushing the daydream from her mind, "I chatted with Sarah Peters last night, an ex-Raven Stone romance author. She's thinking about submitting her manuscript to a small press and would like an editor to help her shine it up. I could pass on your information to her too, if you like."

Matthew placed a glass in the top rack of the appliance. "Really? Dylan's coming over tomorrow to help me with my website. So, maybe next week you could send her my website address. If you don't mind, of course."

"I still don't mind," Anna replied. "I'm the one who thought of it. She would probably leave you a nice testimonial too. Have you heard from Scott yet? He said he wanted to tweak a few plotlines before contacting you."

"Not yet. But hopefully soon." Matthew popped the last plate inside the dishwasher with a clink. "I'd really like to get things rolling. If I could work from home and stick around here—" he glanced at her— "well, I'd rather not move if I don't have to."

Anna's stomach knotted. *I want you to stick close to home too.* She wasn't sure what would happen if he left. Would they try dating long distance? She'd done that before with Jace, and it didn't go well. But Matthew seemed different. She couldn't imagine him running off with another girl.

Matthew closed the appliance's door, then reached down to scratch Monty's ears.

A handsome man who cooked me a stellar meal, and he also happens to be great with my dog? Yep. I definitely don't want him to leave Cedar Lake.

He straightened and caught her eye, then gave her a silly grin. "What?"

"Nothing," Anna replied. "Just wondering what you used in that dressing for the kale and cranberry salad. It was so good. I bet we could use it at the inn."

He shook his head. "It's a Talbot family secret. My mom would kill me if she found out I leaked it."

"Hmm. So, I assume Sophie knows it already, then."

"Nope. Not until she's a Talbot."

All it takes is marriage to get the secret recipe? Anna bit back the words. *Nope, it's way too early to think like that. Even if it is only a joke.*

She got up from the table and joined him in the kitchen area. "Well, I guess I'll have to wait until she marries Marshal. Then I can get the recipe out of her for my own personal use."

Matthew leaned his back against the island and lifted a brow. "Mom will have her swear an oath of secrecy, probably on Marshal's life." He grabbed Anna's hand, and she let him tug her against him.

"I'm sure Marshal is a worthy sacrifice," she teased. "Come on, what is it? I could have sworn there was a touch of apple cider vinegar."

He looked down at her with that crooked grin, his wavy hair slipping over his forehead. The woodsy smell of his cologne filled her with longing, and she fought the desire to run her fingers along the edge of his freshly-shaven jaw. He wrapped his arm around her waist, and she rested her hand on his chest. They were close enough, if she stood on her toes, like that night in front of her door—

Monty pawed at Anna's leg and let out a whine. Startled, she pulled away from Matthew and patted the dog's head, disappointed at the interruption. "Need outside, buddy?"

He let out a low *woof* and trotted to the entrance of the hallway, then looked over his shoulder at them.

Matthew chuckled. "I'd say he needs to go. Stat."

"I'll take him out and make sure he doesn't go on anyone's tires."

Matthew pushed away from the island. "I'll come with you." He rubbed his chin. "Hey, want to see Sophie's new chickens while we're out there?"

"Did you say Sophie's *chickens*?"

Matthew nodded. "Marshal got her some laying hens. They're up in our grandpa's old coop. She doesn't know about them yet. He's going to surprise her on Sunday when they get home."

A wave of humour rolled through Anna. She could envision Sophie cooing over the birds as she collected eggs. "That's cute. She'll love them. She was trying to convince Katie to set up a coop at the inn."

They followed Monty down the hallway to the front porch, and he urgently pushed against the door. Matthew flicked on the outside light. "Is he okay off his leash?"

"Sure, I take him to the off-leash dog park all the time."

He let Monty outside, and Anna turned her back to slip on her shoes.

"Here." Matthew stepped up behind her with her coat in his hands, holding it open.

She gave him a shy smile, then slipped her arms through the sleeves. "Thank you."

They went outside into the cool night air and made their way down the front steps. Anna squinted in the dim light of the yard lamp, looking for Monty. She frowned. "Do you see him anywhere? Usually he doesn't go far."

"He might be behind the bushes, off in the shadows somewhere." Matthew rubbed his hands together. "Monty?" he called out. "Come here, boy!"

Anna listened for the sound of rustling leaves or Monty's padding footsteps. Nothing. "Monty!"

A muffled bark met her ears, and then panicked squawking filled the night air.

Anna and Matthew exchanged glances. He pulled his phone from his pocket, turned on the flashlight, and started across the dark yard. Anna followed behind him, hurrying to keep up with his long strides. "The chickens! You don't think he got inside their coop, do you?"

"I wouldn't be surprised." Matthew's voice was calm. "Chickens make fun targets for dogs. I'm sorry, I should have known better than to let him out without a leash. All the flapping and flying feathers—a chicken coop is like an amusement park for them."

Anna's mouth went dry at his words, and another bark and a cry from an angry chicken floated through the air. Matthew led her around the side of the house, past a firepit area, to a ramshackle shed with peeling shingles with a chicken-wire fence around it.

He flashed the light in the outdoor run area. Sure enough, Monty lunged through the tall, brown grass, on the tail of several snow-white hens.

"Monty! Stop!" Anna cried out.

They rushed through the gate, which Monty had pushed open. Anna scrambled, trying to see him in the dark so she could grab his collar, but it was as if he wasn't even aware of her presence. He had zeroed in on those birds, and nothing else seemed to register in his mind.

Matthew handed Anna his phone, then put his fingers to his lips and let out a shrill whistle. Monty faltered in his stride, and the chickens scurried away from him and scooted through the chicken-sized door into the coop.

Before Monty could follow and stick his big head in there, Matthew grabbed his collar.

"Easy, buddy," he said in a soothing voice. Monty pulled against him half-heartedly and licked his chops. "No chicken dinner for you. Not tonight."

Anna strode to Matthew's side and wrapped her fingers around Monty's collar. "Here, you check the hens and make sure there are no injuries." She returned his phone to him.

Matthew gave her a nod and made his way to the coop. He shone his light through the door, then stepped inside. After a moment, he returned outside and closed the door behind him. "All six are accounted for. There doesn't appear to be any injuries, only some ruffled feathers."

"Thank goodness." Anna let out a sigh of relief. "Monty, what were you thinking?"

"He was just being a dog." Matthew said as he walked back to her. "Like I said earlier, I should have known. I closed their little door to keep them inside for the night." He ruffled Monty's ears. "And I bet I know who's been busting out of the kennel at the inn now. It's not your friend, Mack, is it?"

Monty cocked his head, as if trying to look innocent.

Anna shook her head. "I guess he was tricking us all along with his old man act."

"The innocent-looking ones are usually the perpetrators. Right, boy?" Matthew scratched Monty's neck. "Let's get him up to the house and leashed."

With Anna leading Monty by his collar, they made their way across the lawn and into the circle of the yard light at the house.

Before Anna could get the dog inside, headlights appeared on the driveway.

She looked at Matthew. "Are you expecting anybody else?"

"No," he replied, watching the lights approach. "It's probably Mom. She pops by unannounced once in a while."

Anna's stomach twisted. *His mom? Sophie's going to find out I was here for sure. And Marshal. And Madison.* Was he ready to let his family know they were dating?

A white Honda pulled up in front of the house and parked next to Anna's and Matthew's cars. Anna tightened her grip around Monty's collar so he wouldn't lunge to greet Paula.

"I don't know that car." Matthew cocked his head, his brows knit together.

The door opened and a woman with waist-length blond hair emerged, and his face turned bright red.

She looked them up and down, then righted her leather purse over her shoulder, shut the car door, and strode toward them. "Hello, Matthew. My flight came in early, so I thought I'd come out tonight. I stopped by your parents' place, and they gave me directions to find you here." She slid her gaze to the farmhouse and her eyes widened. "This is where you're living?"

"Hey, Brittany." Matthew frowned and rubbed the back of his neck. "Yeah. I live with Marshal now."

Brittany? The knot in Anna's stomach hardened. Monty pulled on his collar, but she held tight. *His ex. She flew out here to see him.*

Brittany gave Anna a wide, fake smile. "Hi, there. I guess Matthew's not going to introduce us. I'm Brittany. And you are?"

Matthew cut in. "Hey, I was going to—"

"It's okay." Heat swept over Anna's face, but she lifted her chin. "I'm Anna. I've been working with Matthew at the inn."

"Oh, you're Anna?" Brittany flicked her gaze to Matthew. "Is this *the* Anna? The girl with the awesome mountain story you sent to Dana?"

Anna froze, her heart scraping against her ribs. *He what? He sent my manuscript—*

Matthew's frown grew deeper. "How did you know about that?"

"I'm meeting with Dana next week too. We were chatting, and she said she'd talked to you recently." She looked at Anna and tossed her long hair over her shoulder. "She said your first chapters are promising. I'm impressed. It takes a lot to make Dana sit up and take notice."

Anna stared at Matthew, confusion swirling in her mind. *Dana? Promising? What does—wait, he did send it. Without my permission.* "You sent my chapters to that agent already? I asked you if you thought they were ready."

Matthew's eyes widened with surprise. "You said you wanted to take me up on my offer—"

"Once my chapters were ready." Anna tightened her grip on Monty's collar, every fear from the last few months washing over her.

She had practically lost her shot with *The Wicked Moon*, and now she may as well scrap this story too. She hadn't been sure if it was ready, she'd wanted more suggestions first. And now, if Brittany is just blowing steam and this agent doesn't like it—*well, how are two rejections going to look on my resumé? I'm done. My mom was right.*

"Anna, I'm sorry. I must have misunderstood your email. I thought you asked me to send it. And honestly, it's good—"

"It doesn't matter." Anna started toward her car, tugging Monty along with her. "Look, I better take off and let you two catch up."

Brittany turned on her heel, watching Anna stride away. "Well, it was nice to meet you, Anna. Good luck with your book."

"Anna, wait." Matthew started after her, but Anna loaded Monty into the back seat, then opened the driver's side door.

"I'll see you Monday, Matthew," she said, avoiding his gaze. She dipped her head at his ex-girlfriend. *Or is it not-so-ex? Just like Jace. And I thought Matthew was different!* She choked back a sob. "Nice to meet you, Brittany."

Before Matthew could protest again, she slid into her seat, closed the door, and put on her seatbelt. Without looking back, she started the car and reversed onto the driveway.

Monty gave a soft whimper from the back seat as they bounced down the gravel. Anna let out the angry sob she'd been holding. *My career is in tatters. Mom's riding my back about a job and moving home. I almost fell for another jerk guy.* She gripped the steering wheel with white-knuckled fingers. *When am I going to catch a break?*

Chapter Seventeen

Matthew closed the gate to the chicken run, testing the new latch he'd installed. It clicked shut securely, and he rattled the wire to make sure it would hold. Satisfied, he tucked his screwdriver into his back pocket.

His boots crunched over the frost-covered grass as he made his way to the chicken coop, and his breath puffed in the crisp mid-morning air. He opened the man-sized door on the building, letting the warm air wash over him, and poked his head inside. The chickens stared at him from their roosts, making soft clucking noises.

"Good morning, ladies. I'm sorry I kept you literally cooped up in here all day yesterday. That darn dog destroyed your gate." He lowered his voice.

"But don't worry, that nasty scoundrel is gone, and I fixed up your run. I can let you out now."

The closest hen ruffled her feathers and cocked her head, as if she understood.

Is this what it's come to? Talking to chickens? I need a real job, stat. He stepped into the coop and went to the chicken door at the front, unlatched it, and swung it open. With a squawk, what must have been the leader of the flock hopped off her roost and ran outside. Matthew took a step back, and the other hens followed her.

He left the coop and closed the man-door behind him, then leaned his shoulder against the side of the structure to watch the hens rustle through the long grass inside of the fenced-in run. The way they bobbed their heads and scratched at the ground had always amused him, even as a kid. If he remembered the flock his grandfather had years ago correctly, these girls would have their run cleared of grass in a matter of days. That was their job—to eat, scratch, lay in the sun, and let nature take its course.

If only life were so easy. He sighed, his mind reeling with thoughts of Anna and their disastrous date the night before last. They'd been having such a great time, even with Monty's attempt at mass chicken murder.

Cooking dinner, laughing over coffee, hanging out and getting to know each other more—it had all felt so natural. With no pressure to go anywhere or prove anything to anybody, he'd never been so content with someone before. *Why did Brittany have to show up and ruin everything?*

Of course, Anna hadn't answered his call yesterday. And why would she? His ex-girlfriend had shown up at his house, and had obviously made a big effort to do so. It wasn't like she lived down the road, she'd flown all the way out from Toronto. Anna had every right to be suspicious.

But her anger about him sending her chapters to Dana—he had reread her email, and it was clear to him that there had been a miscommunication. She'd stated she wanted to take him up on his offer to send it, but after reading further, he could see now that she'd wanted some reassurance first. It was a boneheaded move on his part, but if he could talk to her and explain, she'd surely understand. Right?

Besides, her chapters were great. She was talented and had a solid hook that any agent searching for inspirational stories would eat up. He'd thought she'd be grateful for the recommendation.

His first reaction to her harsh words had been to defend himself, but in all the emotional chaos he hadn't been able to get a word in before she stormed off. But maybe the time to cool off was a good thing. He'd certainly had time to think yesterday, mulling over how to piece what happened together.

Insensitive... that's what Brittany had called him when she broke things off. He swallowed the lump in his throat. It was true, he hadn't always given much thought to her side of things. And now, was he doing the same thing to Anna, expecting her to be grateful instead of trying to see her view of the situation?

She's raw and worried after what happened with Raven Stone. I broke her trust.

Matthew uncrossed his arms and let out a groan. He watched the hens bopping merrily around the run. "Ladies, what do I do now? What kind of featherly advice do you have for me?"

A woman's laughter met his ears, and he looked in the direction of the house. Marshal and Sophie walked through the yard toward him, their arms entwined. Sophie practically bounced with every step, excitement lacing her voice.

"Chickens, Marsh? This was the last thing I expected!"

Matthew straightened and met them at the gate. "Hey, you two are home early. Have a nice getaway?"

"We did! It was perfect. This guy," Sophie squeezed Marshal's forearm, "even relaxed and didn't talk about work for a second."

"A fireplace and an ice-cold glass of dark ale will do that," Marshal said. He gave her a silly smile. "And of course, sharing it all with you."

Matthew raised his brows, fighting back a laugh. He'd never seen his brother so smitten. At least, not since they were teens, when he'd first fallen for Sophie. But at that time, she'd had no idea.

Sophie blushed. "This morning Marshal broke down and told me he had a surprise for me here. So, I wanted to hit the road right away to find out." She tossed her copper waves over her shoulder, then approached the wire fence and peered at the hens inside. "Just look at them. They're so sweet!"

Matthew flipped the new latch on the gate and opened it.

Marshal's gaze fell on the shiny new metal.

"What happened here?"

Matthew shrugged and gave him a sheepish grin, then stepped out of the run. "Just an incident with a dog. Not a big deal. The birds are fine, and I fixed the gate. Nothing's getting in here now."

Sophie, only half-listening, rushed inside the enclosure to check out the birds. "Oh, poor girls! I hope they weren't too stressed."

Matthew closed the gate behind her. "They seem pretty settled now. I think I saw a few eggs in their nesting boxes, if you want to go look."

Sophie let out an excited squeal, then went into the coop in search of eggs.

"A dog?" Marshal asked. "Whose dog? Did the Wolskys' German shepherd come over here? I should call Greg and let him know about the chickens."

"No, it didn't belong to any neighbours," Matthew replied. "It was Monty, Anna's dog."

"And why was Anna's dog here?"

"Because Anna came over for supper on Friday."

Marshal lifted the brim of his ball cap and rubbed his forehead. "Are you two dating? Look, I don't mean to pry. But if she's going to be around, I'd like to know.

We can add some extra reinforcements to make sure this run is predator proof."

"I don't know. I messed up, and I don't know how to fix it." For the umpteenth time, Matthew remembered the hurt look on Anna's face when she got in her car to leave on Friday, and the ball in his chest grew even tighter. "Brittany showed up while Anna was here."

Marshal let out a low whistle and shook his head. "That is bad."

"Yeah," Matthew replied dryly. "To say the least."

"She flew all the way out here? Why? To get back together?"

Matthew scrubbed his face with his palm. "No, she has a new job in Vancouver for a publishing company. They need a line editor."

"You didn't sign on, did you?"

Matthew shook his head. "Nope. As much as I want a job close by, one thing was made clear last night—I cannot work with her again. I don't even want to try."

"That's good. You shouldn't." Marshal paused and rubbed the back of his neck. "You know, if you talk to Anna—"

"And say what?"

"I dunno, telling her you didn't *invite* your ex-girlfriend to crash your date would probably help."

Matthew pushed back his ballcap and rubbed his temple. "I tried to call her yesterday, but she didn't answer."

"Did you forget where she lives? Or works?"

"I don't want to force her to talk to me if she isn't ready."

Marshal let out a sigh, then crossed his arms. "Okay, you're probably right to give her some space if she isn't ready. But a word of advice—if you really like her, you owe her that explanation once things have cooled down. No matter if you end up together or not, don't leave her thinking you betrayed her." He glanced toward the coop, and his face softened. "And you owe it yourself to make things right with her too. Don't let your stubborn pride get in the way of a good thing."

Matthew's throat thickened. As much as he didn't like to admit it, Marshal had a point. It surprised him how much he hated the fact that he'd hurt Anna. Again. He had to talk to her. Even if she didn't want to pursue a relationship with him, he couldn't leave her bruised over what had happened.

And maybe she'll forgive me. Maybe we can try again.

The coop door banged open, and Sophie stepped out with her hands cupped together, holding several eggs. "Look, Marsh! They're already laying. These are going to be so great for the inn!"

That silly smile returned to Marshal's face. "We'll need a few more hens to keep the inn stocked up on eggs, but I thought six would be a good start for now."

"It's perfect, Marshal. I can't believe you did this for me." She gazed at Marshal, practically batting her lashes as if he were Prince Charming.

Marshal clapped his hand on Matthew's shoulder, then popped the gate latch. "Just talk to her, Mattie." He stepped into the chicken run, and Sophie held out her hands to show him the eggs.

Matthew thought about Marshal's advice, wondering if simply talking to her would really be enough. They had started out with zero trust, and he'd allowed the shaky foundation they had built to crack all over again. *Why didn't I ask her to stay and tell Brittany to leave immediately?* He'd been so shocked at his ex's arrival that he hadn't been able to get the words out.

And because of that, he was about to lose the only woman who'd ever truly liked him for who he was. The one woman who made this town feel like home.

Vanessa's curt tone carried across Anna's apartment, coming from the phone on the coffee table. "I thought you'd be grateful for this opportunity, Anna. It's a full-time job, with benefits and room to grow within the company. You can live with me again and save money to get your own place." She paused. "I'm only trying to help you get on your feet."

Anna let out a frustrated sigh as she buttoned the top to her work tunic. Monty sat at the door, watching her and ready to go. "I know, Mom. I appreciate that you care. But can we talk about this later? I'm trying to get ready for work. It's Sunday, Sophie's night off—"

"And you need to help serve the soup and sandwiches," her mother said. "Yes, I know. I remember you telling me about the casual Sunday nights at the inn before."

"Right. And since it's only Tad and I working, I really can't be late."

"I need an answer tonight. If you don't accept the interview by tomorrow, the HR consultant will assume you're not interested and move on to another applicant."

"Well, consider me not interested, then." Anna strode into her kitchen area and sifted through the junk basket on the counter, pushing aside note pads, pens, a rubber bracelet... "I don't care if the interview the responsible choice. I'm okay for now. I want to make things work out here."

Anna's breath caught. *Did I just say that? To my mother?*

"Excuse me?" Vanessa's voice hitched. "Why? Is it that editor fellow your sister told me about?"

Anna winced. "Kelsey told you about him?"

"In a round-about way, yes."

That traitor.

Her mom continued, "She told me you were doing well out there and had even made some friends. Including him. She told me not to push you. But if I don't, then who else will?"

Guilt pinched Anna's chest. *Okay, not a traitor. But still.* "I don't need to be pushed. I'm overwhelmed enough as it is. But I'm happier here than in Calgary. It's quiet, there's less hustle and bustle, it's better for my creativity. And I have made friends here—"

"Such as this editor. This man."

I'm not getting into this with her. She'd been hiding from her feelings since she woke Saturday morning, determined not to let Matthew and his betrayal get to her. She dove into *The Wicked Moon*, spending hours tearing apart the plotline and character arcs. She rewrote the entire first section, and after going over it a dozen or more times, she sent it to Clarissa that morning.

And as soon as she let her focus drift from her book, thoughts of Friday night came crashing into her like a wave slamming into a cliff face. Her heart cracked again, the image of Brittany strutting toward them fresh in her mind.

I thought he was different. I'd almost fallen for his act. But he's no different than Jace, reeling me along while pining for his ex-girlfriend behind my back. She shook her head. She was done being somebody's back-up plan. And her manuscript—the one she hadn't even named yet. He'd sent it off to some agent without warning.

Why would he do that? What's in it for him? A job referral maybe. Or a percentage of the commission if she bites. Who knows? Who cares.

She blinked back tears, thinking of the night she'd kissed him. It had felt so natural. So right. What had happened? *How could my heart lead me astray again?*

"Anna? Are you still there?"

She ground her teeth and found one of her hairnets in the basket, then shoved it in the front pocket of her tunic. "Yes, Mom. I'm still here. And no, I don't have a thing going on with any man. Not anymore."

Her mom's voice softened. "Oh, dear. Did something happen?"

Anna's throat thickened, and she made her way to the couch and plopped down on it. "It's okay, Mom. Nothing ever really started anyways. He's definitely *not* why I want to stay here."

Monty padded to the couch and rested his head on her knees. She rubbed his ears, thankful for his comfort.

Vanessa cleared her throat. "If there's one thing I know, it's that the Simone women are cursed with men. We only attract the bad ones. Your grandmother.

Your aunt Miranda. Me." She paused. "I was afraid I'd pass it down to you girls too."

Anna rolled her eyes. "There's no such thing as curses, Mom."

She'd never known her father. He'd left shortly after she was born and wanted nothing to do with her or her sister. So, it wasn't like she ever missed him. But she couldn't imagine how hard it had been for her mom to raise two children on her own. Her single motherhood had always been the driving force behind Vanessa's quest for success—to set up a good life for her girls, without the support of a second parent.

"Well, whatever it is, Simone women have terrible luck with men. It's best to focus on looking after yourself."

"Mom—"

"Let me know tonight about the interview, so we can get a video call arranged for this week. Honey, I urge you to rethink this." She hesitated. "I know you want to be an author so badly, but you've said it yourself. It's a tough industry to make a living in. I want you to be financially secure. You're not the only writer struggling to make it."

Anna pressed her fingers to her temple, and Monty scrambled onto the couch and lay next to her. She rested her hand on his back. "Mom, I gotta go. I'll call you later tonight, okay?"

"Okay." Vanessa's voice grew lighter. "You know, it's snowing here. You've always loved the first few snowfalls of the year."

Anna's lips twitched. The early winter snowfalls in Alberta were the one thing she had been missing this year—the wonder of waking up to the dull, brown world transformed into a magical winter wonderland.

"Enjoy it for me. I'll talk to you later."

Her mom said goodbye, and Anna picked up her phone and checked the time. She still had five minutes before she had to get going, but she'd been desperate to end the uncomfortable conversation. *And now I have just enough time to see if Clarissa has responded to my revisions.*

She tapped her email icon, and her stomach quivered at the sight of a new message from her agent. She opened it, anxious to see what the woman had to say.

Hi Anna,

I'm sorry, but I don't think this is it. Rowena still comes across as an adult. You say she's seventeen, but she acts and speaks like she's thirty. I'm going to have to set The Wicked Moon *aside for now. Do you have anything else you're working on? Stories with witches or werewolves are popular right now. I'd love to see something like that.*

Let me know and take care,

Clarissa

Anna blinked, then reread the email. Her vision blurring, she turned off her phone and let the tears fall.

CHAPTER EIGHTEEN

Matthew lifted the last milk can over Marshal's tailgate, then slid it into line with all the others in the truck box. His parents' yard light illuminated their shiny exteriors. He had to admit, they looked pretty good. His mom and her friends had cleaned them up nicely and wrapped white organza sashes around them. The tidy evergreen-coloured bows with fake white roses were the perfect touch.

His mom shuffled out of the shed with a massive cardboard box in her arms. Pussy willow branches with closed red buds poked out from the top. "Don't forget these. We'll stick them in the tops of the cans once they're set up inside the barn."

"Mom, where are your crutches?" He met her and took the box from her.

"They're right there," she gestured toward the crutches leaning against the side of the shed. "Stop worrying so much."

"Start using them, you're going to make your ankle worse." He took the box to the truck and set it on the passenger seat, then closed the door. "What would Dad say if he saw you hobbling around here without them?"

"Alright, stop fussing. I'm the parent here." She pressed her lips together, then grabbed the crutches and swung her way to the vehicle.

Matthew sighed and decided there was no point in arguing with her. "So, tomorrow's the big decorating day, huh? Do you feel like everything you had planned is coming together?"

Paula leaned on her crutches, looking over the canisters one more time. "I think so. Sophie has a buffet table filled with holiday-themed treats planned—our first taste of sugar cookies for the year. We've got hot chocolate and Irish cream for the bar. Marshal is at the barn now, hanging the white lights and drapes."

"Sounds like everything's shaping up for a good night."

She nodded. "You know, your skeleton crew did a great job cleaning up that barn. I hardly recognized it when I walked in there this morning. When I first saw it, I thought Katie was crazy to think it would be ready in less than a month. But you all proved me wrong."

"Turns out I'm not completely useless with a power drill."

"Or a broom," she said with a wry smile. "Hopefully we can have more events there. It's good for the town and for the Starlight Inn too. I bet on Monday the inn's phones will be ringing off the hook with wedding bookings."

"I wouldn't doubt it."

His mom tapped one of her crutches on the gravel at their feet. "How is, umm, Anna, is it? Did she enjoy working on the barn project too?"

Matthew narrowed his eyes at her. "Why do you ask?"

She blinked at him innocently. "Oh, well, Marshal mentioned you were hanging around with her a bit. He said there was an incident with her dog and the chickens."

His throat tightened. Anna had practically ignored him all week while they put the finishing touches on the barn. Every day he'd tried to talk to her so he could apologize for what happened and clear the confusion about Brittany, but as soon as he'd opened his mouth, she'd always had an excuse to leave the room—she'd needed to put away the painting supplies, help Sophie set up the buffet table. She'd even left to check the new gate on the dog kennel. Twice.

He hadn't tried calling her again. She wouldn't answer anyways, and he wanted to speak to her in person. But she was making it impossible. As each day went by, he'd felt worse and worse, mentally torturing himself every time she'd walked by and avoided his gaze.

"You know, Marshal's just as big a gossip as you are."

Paula pursed her lips, looking disappointed. "Aww, hon." She moved beside him and patted his shoulder. "I was hoping you'd found someone nice. Someone to make you happy, like Marshal has with Sophie and Madison with Dylan."

"You've got to stop comparing me to them, especially Marshal," he replied dryly.

"I'm not comparing—"

"You and Dad have always compared me to him. I grew up in his shadow." *What am I doing, opening this can of worms?* But he couldn't stop. "Don't get me wrong, I'm lucky to have him as a brother. For a long time, I tried to be like him, but it never worked. And when I set out to make my own life, you seemed happy."

"We were, dear—"

"Until I lost my job," he said, regretting his curt tone immediately. He rubbed his face with his palm, trying to think of how to word what he wanted to say. "It wasn't my fault, you know. The company folded. It had nothing to do with me or my work ethic."

Paula took a deep breath, her blue eyes misty with tears. "We know that, dear. Your dad and I, we aren't disappointed in *you*. Only with the circumstances. The job loss and the break up, your whole world changing in one week." She swallowed. "When you kids hurt, we do too."

"I never meant to put that on you."

"You don't have to put it on us, it's just how parenting works." She paused. "You might find that out yourself one day."

"Don't get your hopes up. Not any time soon, anyways." He gave her a sideways look, and he caved. "Things with Anna didn't work out. Brittany showed up at the house while she was there."

Paula's face grew pale. "I'm so sorry. I told her where you were, but I didn't know you had a guest over. She said she wanted to talk to you about that job in Vancouver, and you'd told me earlier that you were thinking about it. I thought …" She shook her head sadly. "What happened?"

"It's not your fault," Matthew said with a sigh. "Britanny should have warned me that she was coming. She rolled right in there, as if I'd be happy to see her, and introduced herself to Anna."

"You didn't—well, you didn't accept the job, did you? Right in front of Anna?"

"No, of course not. Besides, Anna took her dog and tore out of there before I had a chance to say anything."

"Oh, Matthew," Paula replied in a hushed tone.

"I'm not taking the job anyways, Mom. I landed my first freelance client this morning." He paused, thinking of the email he'd received from Anna's author friend, Scott. "Somebody Anna suggested me to, actually."

"Oh, that's great news!"

Matthew swallowed the painful lump in his throat. "Anna talked me up to some of her author buddies. And instead of repaying the favour, I—"

"Oh, hon." His mom cocked her head. "If you tell her the truth about what happened that night with Brittany—"

Matthew held up his hand. "That's not the only thing. I broke her trust with her work too. She'd given me her new manuscript to critique, words she'd poured her sweat and tears into. And I misunderstood and sent it off to an agent friend of mine before she felt it was ready. All the while thinking she'd be grateful for my help." He thumped his fist against the side of the truck. "Maybe I *should* try to be more like Marshal. Look how happy he makes Sophie. The man got chickens for her, for crying out loud."

Paula chuckled, then reached out and squeezed his arm. "Do you like this girl?"

"Of course I do. A lot."

"Then fix it."

He turned and leaned his back against the truck. "And how do I do that? You and Dad have been married for thirty years. What's your secret?"

"It's not always sunshine and roses, dear," she replied. "Heaven knows we can drive each other crazy some days." She tilted her head. "But communication is a start. You need to at least talk to her and clear the air about everything that's happened. And if she's open to listening, you better try some honesty too. Let her know how you really feel. I imagine she's confused as all heck right now, with your ex-girlfriend crashing your date."

"And what if she won't listen to me? If she shuts me down every time I say a peep to her and walks away like I'm carrying the plague?"

"Then maybe it wasn't meant to be. And you have to let her go to make room for the right person."

They were quiet for a moment. Matthew chewed on her words, his chest aching, and not feeling any closer to an answer than he was before.

"Just make it clear she matters to you, hon, and see what happens. At least then, you'll know." Paula wiped her hands on her jeans, then gestured toward the house. "Do you want to come inside and chat with Dad?"

Matthew patted the edge of the truck box and shook his head. "No, it's getting late and I better get these to the inn. See you tomorrow?"

"Bright and early," Paula replied. "Oh, would you be able to do me a favour?"

"What's that?"

"Can you ask that Dane fellow, the stable manager, if he's doing hayrides with the horses Saturday at the tree lighting? I sent him an email last week, and he hasn't responded."

"Hayrides?"

"Yes, dear. You know, with horses. And a wagon. Maybe some hay?"

Matthew raised his brows. "You are sassy tonight." He replied, thinking back to his talk with Anna in the horse pasture last week. *She loves sleigh rides.* "And yeah, I'll talk to Dane first thing."

The familiar chimes tinkled above Anna's head as she entered Steeped in Books, enjoying the comforting smell of herbs and new paper. On a mission for more of that green tea Christine had given her, she'd vowed she wouldn't browse the shelves this time. Her temporary part-time job was about to end, and her wallet couldn't take it.

Still, she glanced at the covers as she made her way toward the front counter. A bright cover with a couple entwined in a passionate embrace caught her eye, and she lifted her nose and kept marching. Romance was the last thing on her mind. She was making the most of her free afternoon before the busy weekend. And without having to beat her head against her *Wicked Moon* manuscript now, she could do whatever she wanted.

First up, tea and a nap. She reached the front counter, but Laura was helping a customer in the comic book section. She rang the bell, and Christine came rushing out from the back room.

"Anna! It's so good to see you." She patted her frizzy hair, then narrowed her eyes and looked Anna up and down. "What's wrong?"

Anna forced a chuckle. "What do you mean what's wrong? I'm here for a bit more tea. I drank all the stuff you gave me already. The green jasmine with the rose petals, I loved it."

"Something's wrong. Your energy—it's off."

"Right. Okay." *What am I supposed to say to that? You're right, I lost my agent. I'm probably moving home with my mother. I foolishly fell for another jerk. My life is an even bigger mess than it was before.*

Christine leaned over the counter to peer at her closely. "Oh, dear. It's heartbreak, isn't it? Is it something to do with Marshal's brother?"

Anna's breath caught, and she adjusted the shoulder strap of her tote bag. "Oh, Christine."

"If you don't want to share, you don't have to. But I have something that might help." Christine grabbed one of the brown paper tea bags and turned to browse the tea selections on the shelf behind her. "Here," she took a scoop from a basket on the end of the row, "this one has valerian root in it.

It will bring you restorative sleep and sweet dreams to heal your soul."

Anna pushed her glasses up her nose, watching Christine as she filled the bag with tea leaves. "That's exactly what I need. How did you guess?"

Christine replaced the scoop and bent the top of the bag over, then returned to the till and set the tea on the counter. "You look tired, dear. It's Friday—your afternoon off, right? Some sleep would do you good."

Anna opened the top of the bag and breathed in the alluring scent of valerian and chamomile. "You have no idea. I've barely slept all week." She paused, letting the comforting atmosphere wash over her. "This smell—it's amazing. I feel calmer already. How much do I owe you for this?"

Christine waved her off. "Don't worry about it. I hope it helps."

"You'll end up broke if you keep giving your tea away," Anna replied.

"You can repay me with a signed copy of your book one day." Christine winked.

Anna lowered her gaze and refolded the top of the paper bag. "You'll be waiting a long time for that.

My agent dropped *The Wicked Moon*."

Christine took her hand and patted it. "I'm so sorry, Anna. No wonder you're exhausted."

Tears pushed at the edges of Anna's eyes. She hadn't told anybody yet, not even her sister. It was too raw, especially after what had happened with Matthew. All week, she'd kept her phone in the top drawer of her dresser and avoided everybody's calls. And she hadn't missed the looks Tad and Sophie exchanged while at her shift in the kitchen. Her cheeks burned as she thought back to the last few days. She'd been quiet, barely acknowledging Tad's jokes and Sophie's attempts to engage her in conversation.

How could I be so rude? I need to stop pushing everybody away. I have to apologize to them tomorrow.

Now though, in the comfort of the cozy shop, it was like the floodgates to her emotions had opened. She sniffed. "After how hard I worked, Clarissa still let me go. First, writing the darn book, then rewriting it over and over again to meet her expectations. Did you know I even switched the age group?" She shook her head. "As if this story could have ever taken place while Rowena was a teen."

"She made you do all that work, and then dropped you?"

Anna wiped beneath her eye and nodded. "Yup. Now she wants a whole new book." She took a breath. "And I have one started. But it's not in a genre she's interested in."

In fact, she'd thrown herself into her new story every night that week. For once, she'd had no pressure. No looming deadline or agent's requirements to meet. She'd been able to let her mind wander onto that mountain trail and, at least for a moment, escape the dark reality of her situation.

"And you know what? It's actually good. All the new stuff I wrote this week, it spoke to me. But Matthew—" she pulled her hand from Christine's and made a fist— "I trusted him to help me, and he sent my first three chapters to an agent already! An early draft of them, as if they were ready for critique." Anna swallowed, thinking of Brittany telling her last Friday that the agent had liked the chapters. Had she really meant that? Or was she only trying to smooth over the awkward moment? Anna had been stewing over those words all week, too anxious to put any faith in them. "It could be another hit to my writing resumé."

She ached at the thought of Matthew and his mussed-up hair and stupid dimple. She'd managed to avoid him all week at work, but that didn't mean she hadn't longed to speak with him. But what could she say? Every time he'd walked into that barn, she'd caught herself thinking about his hearty laughter at the book club meeting, their talk in the horse pasture and the way his hazel eyes lit up when she'd approved of the steak he'd cooked for her, and how perfectly she had fit in his arms that moment on the street—when they'd kissed in the light of the streetlamp outside her door.

She flicked her gaze to Christine, sure that the pain on her face was evident. "His ex-girlfriend came to his house while I was there for dinner."

Christine reached across the counter and squeezed her forearm. "I'm not an author, and I've been single for twenty-five years. But I am a decent judge of character, and I've known the Talbots since Matthew was a child. They're good people. And Matthew knows the publishing industry well. If he's willing to share your work with an agent he respects, he must be confident in it."

Anna hadn't thought of it that way before. Her stomach churned as she mulled over Christine's words. *Matthew is a professional. Would he be willing to risk his reputation on a less-than-quality recommendation?*

"Maybe you're right."

"That's not to say you have to make amends with him, but I sensed something special when you two were together. A strong aura, if you believe in that sort of thing."

Anna tilted her head. "An *aura* isn't exactly enough for me."

Christine let out a soft laugh. "That's probably a good thing. But, do you think there might be some miscommunication? I find it's usually better to assume people have good intentions, even if they go about things the wrong way."

Anna bit the inside of her lip. "Maybe. I didn't exactly stick around to talk. He's been trying to speak to me at work, but I've been avoiding him." *Which is not exactly fair, is it?*

"Do you think it would be good to hear him out? To find out what really happened, and how he really feels?"

"At this point, I'm not sure if he'd be willing to. I've given him the cold shoulder all week."

Christine patted her arm again, then pushed the bag of tea into Anna's hand. "Give him some credit. What's the worst that could happen?"

Anna gathered the tea and put it in her tote bag. "Thank you, Christine. For the tea and the kind words."

"Any time." Christine reached beneath the counter and pulled out a rectangular box the size of her hand. A moon and stars were painted on the lid. "If you ever want to do a tarot reading, I'm getting quite good at corresponding with the universe."

Anna giggled and gripped the strap of her tote bag. "I'll think about it. First, I need to make some tea and rest."

"If you change your mind, you know where I'm at."

Anna bade her goodbye and made her way toward the door with footsteps a bit lighter than before. Perhaps she'd misjudged Matthew. She wasn't sure. But how would she know if she never even talked to him about what happened? With both Brittany and her manuscript.

The thought of approaching him made her mouth go dry. But it wasn't fair to keep ignoring him.

Maybe it's time to let down my walls. He deserves the chance to explain himself. And then, at least I'll know if it's right to move on.

As she passed the romance section, she spotted a purple cover in the corner of her eye. She stopped to look at it. The author's name was scrawled across the bottom in ornate lettering. *Celia Saint James. Where do I know that name?* She frowned, then the memory of Matthew's sheepish smile when he explained his love for romance books came back to her.

Anna looked over her shoulder at the front counter. Christine was bent over the clackety till, replacing the receipt tape. "Christine?"

"Yes, dear?"

"How well do you know the works of Celia Saint James?"

When Anna pushed open the door to her apartment, Monty came shuffling from his bed to greet her. She rubbed his ears, then slipped off her jacket and hung it and her tote bag on the hook next to the door.

"Well, Monty." She put her hands on her hips. "Should I check my phone and reconnect with the world?"

The dog let out a low woof, and she made her way to her bedroom with him padding softly behind her. She reached her dresser, but hesitated with her hand on the handle of the top drawer. Monty sat at her feet, watching her intently.

"I can do this. Right, buddy?" Between her mom and Kelsey alone, she was sure she'd missed at least a dozen calls over the last few days. She'd sent her sister a quick email on Monday, letting her know she was too busy with the dance preparations to talk this week. But Kelsey probably didn't buy it.

And Matthew… her heart hitched. She took a deep breath, then pulled open the drawer and snatched her phone from the pile of neatly folded socks. *I wonder if this thing is even still charged?* She hit the home button, and the screen lit up with a glaring red five-percent battery sign.

Well, it's not completely dead. She made her way to her nightstand and plugged the charge cable next to it into the cell. She sat on the edge of her bed, then tapped in her PIN.

Her home screen appeared with dozens of notifications for missed calls, texts, and emails. She scanned the messages, which were mostly from her mother and sister as she'd assumed. Only one missed call from Matthew the day after their disastrous date. That was it.

She chewed her lip, thinking of the way he'd approached her this morning, still with a hopeful look on his face despite her terrible behaviour. *He's been trying to talk to me in person. I can't blame him for not calling.*

The bright red dot on her email icon caught her attention, and she tapped it to see what she'd missed. *Nothing important, that's for sure. Clarissa's already ditched me. What else could be in there other than marketing newsletters?*

But among the familiar senders like Kelsey and the provincial writing guild, a new name stood out. *Dana Turner. Subject: Women's Fiction manuscript.* She stared at the phone, not sure if she was reading correctly. *Dana? As in the agent Matthew sent my chapters to?*

Anna opened the email with trembling fingers and scanned the page.

... You have a great hook here, Miss Simone. I have to say I'm really impressed. I would be interested in seeing a synopsis and working with you further to develop this story. This is something women's fiction publishers are hungry for right now ...

Anna let out a choked sob, happy tears brimming her eyes. Monty leapt onto the bed next to her and bumped her with his nose, his eyes bright with curiosity. She wrapped her arms around his shoulders, letting all her pent-up emotions wash over her.

I should have known he wouldn't have sent my chapters if he didn't think they were ready. She closed her eyes, and she thought of his strong hands around her waist. Her heart twinged with longing. *I need to talk to him. We have to sort this all out.*

Chapter Nineteen

*A*nna crossed her legs beneath the skirt of her black cocktail dress, only half-listening to Laura as she regaled her fellow Page Turner, Sue, with an overview of the latest mystery novel that came in to Steeped in Books. The white lights strung from the barn rafters cast a warm glow over the mingling guests, including the Talbot family, who sat a few tables away.

Anna watched Matthew's back as he chatted with his parents. He was in fine form again tonight, with that now-familiar swoop of his chestnut hair and wearing a blue sports coat and tie. She had been trying to get the courage to approach him all evening, but he was constantly surrounded by his family or other townspeople she didn't recognize.

But even if she caught him alone, what was she going to say? *Hey, Matthew. I was a royal jerk about my manuscript. Let's go talk about our relationship? Or lack there-of.*

She propped her elbow on the table and rested her chin in her hand. To think, she'd even straightened her hair again. And she was going to chicken out. Just to avoid facing Matthew, who was the only reason she'd decided to come. She bit back a groan. *What am I doing? Walk by him. Give him a wave. If he sees me, he's sure to come say hello. Right?* She bit her lip, considering it. But what if she'd blown her chances after being so rude to him all week?

Laura's voice jerked her to attention. "Anna? You okay?"

Anna shot her gaze to the pretty bookstore clerk and tilted her head. "I'm alright. I think I'll go for a walk, though. I need to stretch my legs."

"Would you like me to come? We could hit the dancefloor—"

Anna waved her off. She couldn't think of anything she'd rather do less than dancing in a crowd of people she barely knew. "I might step out for some fresh air to clear my head. Thanks, though."

Sue set down her glass, then shimmied in her seat. "Are you sure? When they play something more upbeat, meet us out there. It'll be fun."

Laura jerked her head toward the DJ stand. "Let's go ask them to switch it up. They've played three country songs in a row. Not that I'm complaining, but I don't exactly have a two-stepping partner."

Sue agreed, then the two women were off on their mission to liven up the music.

Anna pushed back her chair and got to her feet. She smoothed the skirt of her dress, then gathered her purse and began to make her way toward Matthew's table.

Before she could reach it, Marshal and Sophie rushed by her hand-in-hand. Giggling to each other like lovesick teenagers, they didn't even notice her. Anna hesitated as they made their way toward the Talbots. From their table, Matthew's father beckoned at the couple to sit with them.

Heat rushed to Anna's face, and she spun on her heel and strode toward the coat room. *I can't do this. Not here. Not with his family and everybody watching.*

Matthew tapped his fingers on the table in time with the country song pouring from the speakers on the dancefloor. His parents sat next to him, visiting with the couple at the table behind them. He scanned the room, looking for Anna. He hadn't seen her yet tonight.

Marshal and Sophie plopped down in the chairs across from him, laughing and out of breath. Marshal nodded at him, then took a sip of his wine.

Paula leaned in their direction. "Well, you two are sure having fun. Where are Madison and Dylan?"

"Still dancing," Marshal replied. "You know how Madison is. She's going to wear the poor man out."

Matthew glanced at his watch, then looked around the room again. Still no sign of Anna.

Sophie took a breath, her cheeks pink. "She's just about worn *me* out already." She poured herself a glass of water from the jug on the table. "You're quiet tonight, Matthew."

"He always is," Marshal said with a grin. "Social gatherings have never been his thing."

"They aren't yours, either," Matthew replied. "Or at least, they weren't until Sophie came back on the scene."

Marshal glared at him and opened his mouth to retort, but Matthew beat him to it. "Hey, I'm just glad you're in a good mood." He tipped his glass toward Sophie. "You're good for him. Please stick around. For all our sakes."

Sophie laughed again, then squeezed Marshal's arm and his scowl softened. She took a drink of her water, then pointed to the pine centerpiece laced with white roses and baby's breath. A white candle stuck out from the middle of it. "Paula, these decorations are gorgeous. You and your team did a fantastic job."

Paula beamed at her. "Oh, thank you, Sophie. That's sweet of you to say."

Bill nodded and ran his hand through his wavy salt-and-pepper hair, then put his arm around the back of her chair. "You sure did, hon. And that tree lighting—I think it was the best one Cedar Lake has had yet."

Paula sidled her chair closer to her husband. "It was wonderful, wasn't it? Shelley came up with the idea for those candy canes with the notes from Santa for the kids. We hung them on the lower branches of the tree so they could pick their own."

"I'm sorry I missed it," Matthew replied. "I was bogged down here getting everything ready for the dance."

"It sounds like it was a good thing you were here." Marshal glanced up at the overhead heaters Rodger and Matthew had installed in the barn rafters. "I heard the shipment for the heaters came in late."

Matthew took a sip of his wine. "They didn't come in until this morning. We had to scramble to get them up in time. Luckily, we had a lot of help today."

Most of the Starlight Inn staff had pitched in that afternoon with the last-minute details. Sophie, Tad, and Anna had been busy in the kitchen, getting the food and buffet ready. Dane and Ethan had stocked the bar and drink area. Even Madison had come to take over the decorating after their mom left for the ceremony.

And it was all worth it. *The whole town must be here.*

Matthew gazed around the room, recognizing so many faces, from his old high school teachers to the guys from Boy Scouts. Even some of the Page Turners from Christine's book club had shown up. The country tune ended, and a fast-beat pop song pulsed through the air. The dance floor was filled with couples and singles alike.

Marshal's right. I would rather saw off my left leg than get dragged out into that mass of bodies. Anna would agree.

As though the thought were a summoning spell, Anna appeared in the crowd. For a moment, he was taken aback by the slim-fitting black dress she wore. He'd never seen her in anything fancier than jeans and a blouse. He tried to catch her eye, but she turned on her heel and headed toward the coat room.

He set down his glass, then slid back his chair and got to his feet.

Bill gave him a questioning look. "Where are you going, son?"

"I need to check something." Matthew tugged at the collar of his shirt and loosened the top button. "I'll be back in a bit."

Marshal followed his gaze, then gave him a quick nod and a thumbs up.

Matthew took off in the direction she'd gone, hoping she wasn't leaving. He'd been thinking about what to say to her all day, how to apologize and explain what happened with both Brittany and the manuscript. To thank her for helping him land his first freelance editing client. To tell her how he really felt about her. Now that the dance was here, he wouldn't see her again at the inn. The job was over, and he wanted to make things right before she drifted from his life.

He slipped past a couple of teens giggling next to the doorway, then entered the coat room. Anna stood alone in the back corner, buttoning her wool jacket.

She looked at him, her eyes wide, and he swallowed. "Anna, hey. I just—are you leaving?"

She gave him a weak smile. "Hey. Yeah. I don't really know many people here, and I'm tired—"

"Wait," he said, taking a step toward her. "Please. I'd like to talk."

"Here?" She raised her brow, then pulled a scarf from the hanger behind her and wrapped it around her neck. "It's not really private. I'm sure one of the Page Turners is going to waltz in any minute. Laura and Sue are determined to make me dance with them."

"Dancing isn't your thing, is it?"

She shrugged. "Maybe not tonight."

Matthew's stomach churned. *She can't leave. Not yet. Not before—* he strode to Anna's side. "Please, give me a few minutes."

Anna's face softened, and it took every ounce of Matthew's strength to refrain from wrapping his arm around her. She gently touched his forearm. "Matthew, I'm sorry for ignoring you all week. I really am. But maybe we should talk over coffee. Tomorrow, after we clean up here—"

Footsteps sounded behind them. Matthew glanced over his shoulder. Ethan, the stable hand at the inn, stood in the doorway. Relief flooded through him. *Finally!*

Ethan slid his gaze between them, then cleared his throat. "Er—Dane's ready. He's waiting outside for you two."

"Dane?" Anna cocked her head.

Matthew held out his hand to her. "I know you have every right not to trust me, but please? Come with me."

She bit her lip, giving him a questioning look, but then took his hand. "Okay. I'm curious to see what's up your sleeve."

The tension eased from his neck, and he gave her a wide grin. "Okay. Let me grab my jacket. I'm going to need it."

Anna let Matthew lead her around the tables toward the main entrance of the barn, trying to avoid the glances cast in their direction. *What does he have planned? And what does this have to do with Dane?*

As they strode past the Talbot table, she didn't miss the way Paula and Madison turned their heads, following them with curious gazes. The two women turned to each other and began to whisper, and Anna's heart raked against her ribs. *They must know something's going on with Matthew and I. Do they know about our fight? About what a jerk I was to him this week?*

She paused for a moment, battling the desire to race back to the coat room.

Matthew looked over his shoulder at her and winked, and her stomach filled with butterflies. *It's okay. He doesn't care if they see us together, why should I?* She reached in her pocket and slipped on her gloves, then gave him a slight smile and continued to follow him toward the door.

As they rounded the table nearest the door, she bumped into Tad's shoulder.

"Hey!" He steadied her with his hands, then a mischievous grin crossed his face. "Oh, Anna. Don't let me make you late for your—"

"Hey, Tad." Matthew darted a warning glance at him.

Anna straightened her purse strap over her shoulder and shifted her gaze between them, confused. "Late? For what?"

Tad's grin grew wider, and he bobbed his head. "Right. It's nothing. Just stick with Matthew." He leaned closer to her and wiggled his eyebrows. "Enjoy the ride."

Matthew let out a huff. "Tad!"

Anna shook her head incredulously. "You're both being weird."

"Go on." Tad shooed her toward Matthew, then took off through the crowd of people.

When she stepped outside the stifling barn with Matthew, the frigid air cooled her warm cheeks. A dappled grey gelding pulling a two-person carriage trotted up the lantern-lined walkway and came a stop in front of them. Dane sat in the driver's seat, holding the reins with his shoulders hunched against the cold in his canvas jacket. He tipped his cowboy hat in their direction.

Anna's throat thickened, and she grabbed Matthew's hand. "You—did you set this up?"

He grinned down at her. "I did. I took a lesson from Madison's romance books. And let me tell you, Dane wasn't easy to convince."

Dane chuckled and twisted to look at them. "I only refused until I heard it was for you, Anna. Now, you two getting in or what?"

Anna practically bounced toward the carriage, memories of Christmas sleigh rides at the stable in Alberta washing over her. Sure, they were in BC and there was no snow on the ground—but this was just as magical.

Matthew helped her up the steps, then slid in next to her and pulled a wool blanket from beneath the seat and set it across their laps. "Warm enough?"

"Definitely." Anna couldn't stop smiling. "I can't believe you're bribing me to talk to you with a carriage ride." She paused, thinking of their chat in the field behind the barn, with the horses snoozing beneath the trees. "You remembered."

"I did. Is my bribe working?"

A slow grin crept over her face. "What do you think? Let's go!"

Dane clucked to the horse, and they started toward the trail in the wooded pastures the inn used for wagon and horseback rides for the guests. The moon was almost full, illuminating the hills and the trees around them.

After a few minutes of listening to the soothing sound of the horse's hoofbeats, Matthew craned his neck to give her a serious look. "I owe you an apology, Anna. I should have explained to you what was going on when Brittany showed up like that. I can't imagine how you felt."

Anna's back stiffened, but she gave him a nod. "I'm not going to lie to you, it was terrible."

He cringed. "I know. And I'm sorry. But she didn't come to reconcile. She has a new job for a publisher in Vancouver, and they're looking for an editor. She was trying to get me on board." He paused. "Apparently, there's an employee referral bonus. And she wants it."

Anna's mouth went dry. "A job? In Vancouver?" Her stomach knotted at the thought of him moving away. *Calm down. It's not like you're even dating him. Right? Or is this a date now?*

"Yeah," he said. "It sounds like a great job, but I can't work with her. And the thought of her using me for a referral bonus doesn't sit right. Not after she dumped me by text message."

The tightness in Anna's chest eased away, and she smoothed the blanket on their lap. "She dumped you by text? That's cold."

"Really cold," Matthew agreed. "Besides, I signed an editing contract with your friend Scott. Between that and Dylan helping me fix my website, my freelance gig is starting to roll." He paused. "Thank you for referring me to him and your other friends. Without your help—"

She shook her head. "It's nothing. I'm so glad he reached out. I hope my romance author friend, Sarah, does too. Really, I wouldn't have recommended you if I didn't think you were great. Your notes on my mountain story—"

"About that. And Dana."

Anna let out a groan, then waved him off. "I overreacted, and I'm sorry. I reread my email, and it did seem like I told you to send it." She thought of Christine's words at the book shop—*if he's willing to share your work with an agent he respects, he must be confident in it*. She bit the side of her cheek. "I should have known you wouldn't send my chapters to anybody if you didn't think they were ready. I don't know what I was thinking, getting angry like that."

The carriage bounced over a rock, and Matthew shifted and tucked the blanket tighter around them. "You'd just had your book contract cancelled. By me. I get it—I wasn't the first person you would trust with your work. Next time, I'll make sure we're on the same page before I send your writing off to somebody else."

"Next time?"

"I mean, if you want to work with me again."

"Of course I do." She tucked her arm through his and leaned against him. The woodsy scent of his aftershave wafted over her, and she resisted the urge to snuggle in closer. "I don't want to get my hopes up, but I might not need your help for a while. Dana asked for my synopsis. I sent it to her last night and should hear from her again next week."

"Anna, that's amazing! I knew she'd love that scene on the steep ridge."

This is all going too well. How do I deserve this? After I avoided him all week! Her heart wrenched at the thought of how she'd treated him. His lips curved with a smile, and she remembered the soft taste of them that night beneath the streetlamp.

"Matthew, I'm so sorry I ignored you. I was embarrassed, but that's no excuse. I should have talked to you right away."

"Well," he said slowly. "You could make it up to me with another date."

"A date? That's it? I was thinking of suggesting your editing skills to some more of my writing friends—"

"I wouldn't say no to that!"

Anna pulled her purse onto her lap and opened it. "I almost forgot. I brought a peace offering for you—"

Matthew cocked his head. "You didn't need to do that."

She pulled out the purple romance book with *Celia Saint James* scrawled across the cover and handed it to him. "I doubt it's the same one you read as a teen. She has dozens of books! But, it's purple. And she's the correct author, right?"

Matthew brows rose nearly to his hairline. He turned the book over with an amused look on his face. "This is awesome. I can't believe of all the things I told you, this is what you remembered." He barked a laugh. "A true book nerd. I can't wait to read it. Thank you."

"Maybe we can suggest it for the next Page Tuners read."

"That sounds like a great idea," he replied. "Do you mind keeping it in your purse for now? It won't fit in my jacket pocket, and if Marshal were to find it—"

"Of course." She giggled, then took the book from him and tucked it back in her purse. Right after she closed the zipper, a tiny pinprick of cold landed on the tip of her nose and she gasped. "Was that just—"

"Snow." Matthew pulled his arm from hers and wrapped it around her shoulder, sending a warm tingle through her body. The carriage creaked over the ground, and the air grew colder.

Anna looked up at him, her pulse thrumming inside her, and he pulled her closer. A snowflake landed on his cheek, and she sighed dreamily and snuggled into his side, feeling like the heroine in one of her stories. "Do you think we should try it again?"

Matthew bent his head toward her, searching her face for consent. "Try what again?"

"This." She tilted her chin, and his lips met hers, causing all the pain and anxiety of the last week to melt away.

Chapter Twenty

"He organized a carriage ride for you?" Kelsey's voice was high in Anna's ear. "Like, as in a real horse? And a carriage? With wheels?"

Anna giggled and checked over her shoulder to make sure nobody was listening. With her free hand, she tucked her gloves in the pocket of her jacket, which now hung before her in the coat room of the barn. She and Matthew had just returned to the dance when Kelsey had called, the ringer barely audible above the noise of the music.

"Yes, a real horse." Anna switched her phone to her other ear. "And last I checked, all carriages had wheels."

"That's amazing. Truly, Anna. What a gesture!"

"You sound like you're swooning more than I am." Anna's stomach was still jittery, thinking of the delicate snow and their kiss beneath the moonlight. *Yes, I am definitely a romance heroine tonight.* "Anyways, why did you call? It's Saturday night, I thought you'd be out on the town."

"I'm not feeling well. Besides, I have zero prospects for a date. I have to live vicariously through you."

"Well, that's disappointing. No good men left in Calgary?"

"Not a one," Kelsey replied. "But I called for a reason. Are you still coming home for Christmas?"

"I was planning on it. Mom's pushing for me to move home earlier though." Anna's neck stiffened at the thought. *No, there's no way I'm taking that job or leaving Cedar Lake. Not any time soon.* She would find another part-time job. Even if it meant serving coffee, she was willing to do it in order to stay.

"I had an idea—"

Anna's phone vibrated in her hand. She pulled it away from her ear and frowned at the screen. The word *Mom* blinked at her in flashing letters, the lines of the *M* reminding Anna of furrowed brows. "Oh, Kels. I'm sorry. I better take this. It's Mom."

"Have you told her you aren't taking the interview?"

"Yes. But I have a feeling I'm going to have to again."

"Good luck. I'm sending you all my moral support."

"Thank you. Talk to you later." Anna switched the phone to her mother's call. "Hi, Mom. I'm kind of busy right now."

"Is that music I hear?" Vanessa sounded surprised. "Are you out at a club?"

"No, I'm at the barn dance." Anna stepped aside as a woman in a knee-length red dress entered the room to gather her coat.

"The barn dance?"

The woman glanced at Anna, and Anna lowered her voice. "You know, Mom. I told you I was helping the inn get this barn ready for a community dance."

"Oh, that's right. Well, that sounds cute."

"It is," Anna replied. "So, if I could call you tomorrow—"

"One thing, first. I promise it's quick," Vanessa said. "I emailed you an interview package. It has sample questions for what they might ask on Wednesday, and I thought tomorrow I could help you go through it. We could practice, ease your nerves."

Anna bit back a groan. *She's not going to let this go, is she?* "Mom. Please listen to me."

"Anna—"

"I appreciate all the help you've given me. I truly do." She took a deep breath. "But I'm staying in Cedar Lake. At least for now. I can focus on my writing here. Even it means being broke for a bit. I can get by." She paused, hoping her next words would sound firm. "I'm not going to interview for that job with King Construction."

The phone went silent, and Anna's stomach clenched. "Mom?"

"I heard you."

Was that a quiver in her voice?

"Okay." Anna softened her tone. "I'm sorry to disappoint you, Mom. But this is what's best for me. For now, anyways."

"You're not disappointing me, dear," Vanessa replied with a sigh. "Of course, I would love to have you home. But you've always been dedicated to your writing. And for that, I admire you."

"You do?"

"Your sister told me how hard you've been working on your book. I'm proud of you." Vanessa's voice grew firmer. "But if you're dead set on staying in that little town, then at least let me help you come up with a plan to make it work."

"Sure," Anna replied. "Thank you, Mom."

Matthew stepped into the room. He gave her a wave, then tucked his hands into the pockets of his dark-wash jeans and waited by the door.

"Mom, I gotta go. I'll call you tomorrow, okay?"

"Alright. Enjoy your barn dance."

"I will. Bye." She hung up the call, put her phone on *Do Not Disturb*, and shoved it in her purse. *No more distractions.*

"Sorry if I interrupted," Matthew said. He gestured toward the dance floor. "They're about to play the last dance. And I know dancing might not be your thing—I mean, it's not mine either—but it could be fun. With you."

Anna grabbed his hand and tugged him from the room. "You know, I've never even been to a barn dance before. I guess I shouldn't leave without actually dancing."

"And I'm the lucky guy who gets to escort you?"

"Of course," she said with a grin. "Unless you'd rather I ask Rodger or Tad. Maybe Ethan?"

"No, I'm good. More than happy to be of service."

Matthew guided her through the tables and onto the wooden dance floor. She turned to face him and put her hands on his broad shoulders as the slow dance floated over the room. She sighed happily, spotting Madison and Dylan in a warm embrace on the other side of the room. Tad and Ethan stood together with Tad's parents, laughing at some joke Tad probably made. And Marshal and Sophie, snuggled together at their table with her head on his shoulder.

Anna's heart settled, the calm of the room and the song washing over her. The feel of Matthew's arms around her waist. *This is what's really important. Not deadlines. Not tearing my brain apart trying to rewrite a novel to somebody else's standards. Not money or ex-girlfriend drama or arguing with Mom.*

Matthew gazed down at her. "You look happy. What are you thinking about?"

Anna let out a contented sigh. "That everything's going to be okay, here in Cedar Lake."

"More than okay," Matthew agreed. "I have a feeling that after today, it's going to be a whole new chapter."

"I like that," Anna replied. "The first chapter in the story of us."

Epilogue

Anna folded the burgundy napkin in her hands and placed it inside the box on the table before her. It was the morning after the Starlight Dance, and she'd come in to help clean up the barn. Tad stood next to her, watching the flurry of activity around them as he untangled a string of lights to wrap up properly.

Matthew stood on a ladder near the barn's entrance, taking down some of the white drapes from the rafters. Anna gazed at him longingly and picked up another napkin. By the time she'd arrived about an hour ago, he'd already been hard at work so she hadn't had a chance to say hi to him yet. As soon as she'd walked through the door, Katie had handed her the box and asked her to clear the tables.

But she yearned to talk to him, and the sooner the better. After reading the email she'd found in her inbox that morning, she could barely contain her excitement.

"Anna," Tad's voice grabbed her attention, "you know those are going to be washed, right? There's no need to fold them. Just toss all the table linens in the box, and I'll run them up to the inn later to throw in the wash."

Should I tell Tad about the email? The desire to share her news bubbled inside her, but she couldn't bear the thought of telling anybody other than Matthew first. No, she'd wait.

"Right. Of course these are heading for the wash." Her face warmed, and she shook out the napkin and tossed it inside the box. "Sorry."

"It's fine." Tad tilted his head toward Matthew, who lowered the corner of a drape from above his head. "You're all googly-eyed over Mr. Pompous Editor this morning." He gave her a smug grin. "Not that I blame you. Setting up that carriage ride—a real Fitzwilliam Darcy move."

Anna let out a happy sigh and rested her hands on the edge of the box. "Jane Austen would be impressed."

She turned her gaze to Tad. "How did you know about it, anyways?"

"Ethan told me." Tad began to wrap the light string in a tidy bundle, a goofy smile on his face. "There's no way he could keep something that big a secret. Besides, I saw Matthew talking to Dane and was curious so I prodded it out of him."

Anna raised a brow. "Yes, you two seem to be doing well. I saw you both chatting with your parents last night, like an official couple."

Tad gave her an amused look, then placed the lights in the box at his feet and picked up another string from the table. "Mom said she figured something was going on between us all along, but she didn't want to say anything until I was ready."

"Aww." Anna reached over and squeezed his arm. "Of course she knew. She's your mother." She paused. "I suppose this means more hockey games are in your future?"

Tad rolled his eyes. "I guess so. The things I'll put up with for a cute guy …"

Anna giggled and went to pick up another napkin, but her phone vibrated in her pocket. She pulled it out instead. "It's Kelsey. I should take this."

Tad gave her nod, and she stepped aside to the quiet back corner of the barn to take the call. "Hey, Kelsey. What's up?"

Her sister's cheery tone met her ear. "Get your jingle bells ready, because I'm coming for Christmas!"

"My what? Jingle bells?" Anna cocked her head. "Wait—you're coming out *here*? For *Christmas*?"

"Uh huh," Kelsey replied. "Mom talked to your boss at the inn and booked us a cabin!" The glee in her voice was palpable. "We'll be there from the fifteenth to the twenty-ninth. Two whole weeks of warm BC weather!"

Anna chuckled. "Well, I wouldn't call it *warm* exactly—"

"It's a lot warmer than Calgary's minus twenty, and I assume there's no waist-deep snow drifts."

"True," Anna replied, her mind reeling. Her mom and sister, here in Cedar Lake. A Simone Christmas in a cozy cabin at the inn! She let out a little squeal. "Kelsey! I can't believe you talked Mom into this. I can't wait to show you both around Cedar Lake! And the inn. And the bookstore. You'll get to meet Katie and Christine…"

"And Matthew?" Kelsey asked with a teasing tone.

Anna stomach quivered. "Yes, and Matthew. Oh my goodness, Kels. This is going to be amazing!"

"I know. I've already started packing," Kelsey replied. "But anyways, I'll call you again later with more details. I have to run to meet Mom at the mall for Christmas shopping. She said she'd make sure to join us tomorrow for our virtual dinner so we can start planning."

"Sounds good. Looking forward to it."

They said goodbye, and Anna pocketed her phone. She went to return to the table to finish clearing it, but Matthew was walking in her direction and gave her a wave.

Yes! Now I can tell him my news! She met him near the DJ stand that stood in disarray, partially packed in boxes. "Matthew! I have something to tell you—"

He held out his hand to her, then nodded his head toward the back door of the barn. "Want to take a little break outside to tell me?" His eyes brightened. "It's snowing again."

Anna took his hand. "Like really snowing? Or just a flurry like last night?"

"Really snowing," he replied. "For Cedar Lake, anyways."

"Let's go!" She followed him out the back entrance and into the horse pasture where he'd first asked her on a real date. Big fluffy snowflakes drifted down the sky and landed softly around them, and her breath caught. Two horses stood grazing nearby, a light dusting of snow on their winter coats. "It is snowing. For real."

Matthew nodded and slipped his arm around her waist. "It is. It won't stick around long, but it's pretty while it lasts." He paused, looking down at her. "Now, what do you have to tell me?"

Anna tore her gaze from the snow falling gently onto the horses' backs, then twisted to face him. "Dana emailed me again already. Apparently, she works weekends."

Matthew lifted a brow, grinning. "Only when she's excited about something…"

A spark of joy lit inside her, and she placed a trembling hand on his chest. "Matthew, she loved my synopsis for the mountain story and wants to sign with me. She thinks she's even found a publisher who would be interested. We're going to start working on a pitch this week!"

"Ha!" Matthew let out a hearty laugh, then put both arms around her and hugged her tight. "I knew she'd love it! Anna, that's such great news. Your whole future—it's going to change."

"I know." Happy tears brimmed Anna's eyes, and she hugged him back. The warmth from his body melted into her. "Everything's right again. No, it's even better than before. My writing, my career," she glanced up at him, "you…"

Matthew gazed down at her, then pushed the hair from her forehead, much like he did that night on the street outside her door. "It looks like this chapter is shaping up to be pretty good."

"The best one yet." Her heart warmed, and the snowfall picked up around them.

He bent his head toward her, but before their lips could meet, raucous barking filled the pasture. Anna peered around Matthew's shoulder. Mack bounded toward them with Monty shuffling behind him, their tongues hanging out with the thrill of their freedom.

Matthew let out a groan. "They're out again? I thought Dane and Madison fixed the gate."

Anna started laughing as the dogs reached them, bounding and shaking their soaking wet coats. "Oh, Monty. How are we going to contain you?" She looked at Matthew, who chuckled as Mack bumped into him. "Are you sure you want to stick around and put up with this chaos?"

He picked up a stick from the grass at their feet and threw it over Mack's head. The Great Dane charged after it, his long legs eating up the ground. Matthew shot her that familiar crooked grin, then bent to scratch Monty's scruffy ears. "I can't think of anything else I'd rather do."

If you enjoyed Anna and Mattew's journey to reclaim their love, you can read Sophie and Marshal's love story, ***Pumpkin Promises***, at:

www.jessicarenwickauthor.com

This novella is **FREE** in digital form for newsletter subscribers and has all the romance and fun that *the Starlight Inn* has to offer.

Can a Christmas trip to the Starlight Inn help Kelsey heal her wounded heart?

You can check out Kelsey and Dane's story in ***Starlight Inn Book Three***: ***Holiday Hopes.***

Available at my website, Amazon, Barnes & Noble, and other book retailers.

About the Author

An avid reader and writer since she was a child, Jessica Anne Renwick loves to write cozy stories with themes about family, friendship, and of course—romance! She is also the author of the award-winning children's fantasy series, Starfell.

She is a domestic violence survivor, now living her own happily-ever-after with the man of her dreams. She always enjoys a hot cup of tea, gardening, animals, consuming an entire novel in one sitting, nerding out with video games, and real-life mountain adventures. She resides in Alberta, Canada on a cozy urban homestead with her loving partner, fluffy backyard farm dogs, four chickens, and an enchanted garden.

You can find her at www.jessicarenwickauthor.com, on Instagram @jessicarenwickauthor, Facebook, GoodReads, and BookBub.

www.ingramcontent.com/pod-product-compliance
Lightning Source LLC
LaVergne TN
LVHW040042080526
838202LV00045B/3450